Newcastle Libraries and Information Service

 0845 002 0336

Due for return	Due for return	Due for return
. . . .	. . . .	. . . .
. . . .	. . . .	. . . .
. . . .	. . . .	. . . .
. . . .	. . . .	. . . .
. . . .	. . . .	. . . .
. . . .	. . . .	. . . .
. . . .	. . . .	. . . .
. . . .	. . . .	. . . .
. . . .	. . . .	. . . .
. . . .	. . . .	. . . .

Please return this item to any of N
date shown above. If not requested
can be renewed, you can do this
Charges may be mad

D1350180

ALSO BY LAURINDA D. BROWN

UnderCover

Fire & Brimstone

The HIGHEST PRICE FORPASSION

LAURINDA D. BROWN

SBI

STREBOR BOOKS

NEW YORK LONDON TORONTO SYDNEY

Strebor Books
P.O. Box 6505
Largo, MD 20792
http://www.streborbooks.com

ISBN-13 978-1-59309-053-1
ISBN-10   1-59309-053-6
LCCN 2005920450

Jacket design: © www.mariondesigns.com

First Strebor Books trade paperback edition August 2008

10   9   8   7   6   5   4   3   2   1

Manufactured in the United States of America

For information regarding special discounts for bulk purchases, please contact Simon & Schuster Special Sales at 1-800-456-6798 or business@simonandschuster.com

For Charlotte

ACKNOWLEDGMENTS

Giving thanks to God is like breathing for me. It is something I have to do. I'm walking the path He chose for me, and, as long as I do that, everything in this life is easy. Since I began doing what I was chosen to do, I've removed the word "if" from my vocabulary and replaced it with "when." I've some stopped asking "Why?" and have simply learned to deal with "it" no matter whom or what "it" is. I don't even choose my battles anymore. In my spirit, I know no weapon formed against me has a chance at prospering; therefore, I face everything head on, wearing a suit of armor chosen by God.

Over the past several years of my life, I have put some awful things out in to the universe. Without owning up to any one thing in particular, I will say that most of those things have found their way back to me. Whether it be through the actions of family, friends, or foes, I've been getting that crap back, and instead of walking around tripping about it and insisting everybody has it in for me, I simply shake my head, softly chuckle to myself, and consider it a lesson learned. In turn, I have put some very good things out there, and I am beginning to see those things come back as well.

Writing about life the way in which I have, and keeping friends, is something you have to be anointed to do. Ms. Vicki, a good friend of mine that I met while trying to sell my very first printing of *Fire & Brimstone*, once told me, "Laurinda, you sure have taken a lot of risks for our community; putting our shit all out there in the open." For a second, I felt like I'd betrayed my intimate relationship with the community because I'd exposed our bedroom secrets and touched upon that "taboo" thing that has a tendency to alienate us from our families. Tears welled up in my eyes, and before I could get the apology out, she pulled me to her and said, "Thank you. It's about time somebody did."

During my travels, I have had so many women come up to me thanking me for speaking their words and their truths. Many of them in tears, and some even trembling because I've touched a nerve, brought about a much-needed literary orgasm, or awakened a painful memory they'd put to rest in childhood or at some other vulnerable time in their lives. All I have ever been able to do is reach out, give them a great, big hug, and whisper in their ears, "It's going to be alright, but you have to believe it."

My daughters, Jhoilan and Cydney, breathe life into me. They support me in everything I do, and they are able to make me smile when the rest of the world has gotten under my skin. Throughout this entire project, they have helped me with research, and I have been truly impressed with the knowledge about our history we have each gained. I love them, with everything in me.

Charlotte, my partner of twelve years, has given me the strength and encouragement to do many things; the most important being simply living day by day. She hears about my books when they are merely thoughts and dreams, and she is the first to see them when they are reality. While I've slept through the night, she's stayed up to do my first edits and to give me my first critique. Since we've been together, she and I have seen love come and go for many of our friends, and yet our friendship—because that's what it had to be first—and love have remained true. Yes, we've had issues, but even when I haven't been able to see beyond the moment, she has believed in me and in us.

Shannon, everybody needs someone like her. As my assistant, she has had to endure my hectic schedule and has never been afraid to tell me when I need to slow down. She's been cursed at, fussed at, and yelled at, and she finally got tired and started giving all of that madness back to me. (Well, I guess she told me!) As my friend, she has encouraged me to begin to see myself as others view me. I do it because I love to share stories and experiences to which others can relate. God did a good thing when He sent her to me. Day by day, we continue to learn each other, and we have both grown since our initial introduction. I am thankful for her and her amazing gift of being a great listener.

Zane, I thank her ever so much for being patient with me and this process, which is long overdue. She has believed in me and my unique gift of storytelling and that has meant the world to me. Many times I have nearly completed this book but have been unhappy with what I had, so I started over every single time.

Kathleen, this remarkable woman has never judged me and has allowed me to be who I am. She has never hesitated to tell me when I'm wrong, and I have hurried to correct myself when she's gotten on my case. Both of my children have pictures of her and her husband that they proudly display in their rooms. They don't even have pictures of me sitting around like that. You are truly a blessing from above, and I love you.

Jay and Robin, my sorors, are my confidantes in the "life." We share so many things on a daily basis, and they inspire me to be the best I can be. Embracing the sisterhood in our journey, I cherish every single moment that we spend together. We have a bond to never be broken.

Thomas, this man is one talented individual. Whenever I have needed an ear or a few words of encouragement, he has been right there. Our friendship extends far beyond the norm, as he is truly my brother in ink.

Lastly, I want to thank my bankers—Cynthia V., Cynthia P, and Roger J. All of you know what you have done for me over the years, and I am eternally grateful to you.

Well, I'm done.

Until the next time,

LDB

Straddlin' missus lap with her head pressed against
   my chest
I hear the voices of the slave catchers
Hooves of the horses beatin' against the earth below
My heart runs with them as she touches my breast.

Missus's hands glide 'cross my skin like molasses
   from a tree
She breathes like a bull runnin' wild
Tearin' into my flesh with her tongue
She whispers empty promises to set me free.

Up against her I move with the fire nobody but the
   devil put in my soul
I try to fight her but I can't win
With soft kisses against my neck
Missus reminds me who is in control.

With her spirit wrapped 'round me
I feel somethin' that make her feel almost human
   to me.
But she give that to me like rations
She say when and she say where
The love starts and where it end.

The only thing I have that is truly my own
Is the name my mother gave me.
Missus asked me if I would bleed for it
Her nails buried in me like the whip
Crackin' my flesh leavin' me scarred forever
Then one night while the devil danced in the
  moonlight
Missus, whose skin was both pale and ashen,
Stripped life from me by telling me
My name is Passion.

PROLOGUE

Amelia

The way I am about to tell this story is the way Mother told me to tell it if I were ever asked, and, quite frankly, I never thought anyone would ask. From the first moment I could conceptualize a thought and make a statement of it, Mother taught me to always tell the truth and to never be ashamed of whom I was. On the day she died I felt compelled to tell her about the two times in my life when I was ashamed of whom I was, and while I watched life quietly creep from her body, she calmly asked me to share those experiences with her. Watching her chest rise and fall with more time between each breath, I tearfully opened up my soul to her and told her of deeds that only God had seen. "Amelia, dear," she softly struggled in her warm voice that measured its volume in a soft whisper. "He's already forgiven you and so have I. I love you." A very short time later, Mother's eyes rested upon me for the last time.

Until the very end, Mother encouraged me to believe there were others like me and to recognize that my journey in this life was already laid out for me. A devastating reality for me was that if it were discovered who I was, my life could end in a split second with no time for a last thought or a dying wish.

From the day I was born until now, I have seen people kill for passion—brother against brother, friend against foe. As I grew into my own and learned to love, I realized people live and die for passion, too.

I

During the mid 1700s, by the age of thirty-five, Ambrose Few had become a well-established lawyer in England, but he began to fall on hard times when the economy took a downward turn. With only two paying clients on his ledger, he moved his young wife, Penny, and two children, Litton and June, from England to Baltimore, Maryland and took residence with his Uncle William Few. His hopes of reuniting with his father, Sheldon, were dashed when, upon his arrival, Ambrose discovered that his father and his grandfather, Timothy, had moved to North Carolina to seek better opportunities. Shortly after their arrival in the Carolinas, Timothy and Sheldon began associating with The Regulators, a group of frontiersmen who were against the royal governor. From afar, William encouraged their relationship with the group, although he had no idea what the implications of that involvement could bring. It was not long, however, until he found out. Before Sheldon and Timothy could send for the rest of the family to join them, Sheldon was hanged, and what was to have been the family farm was destroyed by fire. The year was 1771. Feeling responsible for the death of his son, Timothy fled to Augusta, Georgia to try once again to start anew and find a fresh life for his family. In 1776, William Few moved South with his father and began a law practice. He later became one of the signers of the United States Constitution in 1787.

Amidst the constant changes with his family, Ambrose chose to stay in Baltimore for a while to see if he could build his own law practice. As Litton and June grew older, Ambrose and Penny took special pains to ensure that their children developed and maintained their English customs. Penny, a seamstress while in London, had educated her children on the uniqueness and patterns of fabrics as well as the workmanship in fine woods such as mahogany and cherry. When finances would allow, Ambrose would treat the family to Parisian trips so that Penny could purchase needed materials for her business. She took pride in what she did, and no matter where they lived, she knew she could open up shop. One afternoon, while she was picking up thread and needles from the general store, Penny met a young gal who was sitting on the steps right outside the back door. During the day, Penny often took the back exit from the store because it was the shortcut to her dress shop. Dark like the color of scalded chocolate, the young gal was stitching what appeared to be a hem in her dress. Penny's short glances at the woman grew into longer gazes as she kept her pace and headed toward the landing of her shop. She went inside, placed her bags down, and looked out the back window; never letting the gal out of her site.

Two hours passed. Usually, Penny prepared Ambrose's lunch and took it to him at his office, which was right next door. But, on this day, she did not. The gal was still sitting on the back steps of the general store, placing a hem in her dress. Penny could not take it anymore. She needed to see what that hem looked like. For years, she had tried to teach June how to sew, and that child couldn't thread a needle; even if the eye was the size of the sun. Now that her business was flourishing, it was important for her to find suitable help, and she needed someone with the skills possessed by the young gal. Penny, who didn't believe in slavery or the cruelty behind it, made it a point to keep her English manners about her at all times.

Opening the shop's back door, she said, "Pardon me, miss," in a friendly voice from a comfortable distance.

Looking up from her task in which she had been heavily engrossed, the gal looked around to see if a mistake had been made. While she recognized and appreciated Penny's mannerisms, she remembered her own; dropping the bottom of her dress and rising to her feet. "Yessum, miss," she responded with her head lowered to the ground.

Penny had met only one other Negro since she had been in Baltimore, and he—his name was Quincy—occasionally did odd jobs for Ambrose. Walking down the steps and approaching the gal, Penny bent over and reached for the bottom of the gal's dress. "May I?" she paused and asked before lifting the dress up to see the hem.

With a quick nod and bow, the gal replied, "Yessum, ma'am."

"What you got there?" she asked.

"Ma'am?" the gal asked.

Penny lifted the hem of the garment and shook her head in amazement. "You did this?"

"Yessum, ma'am."

"All by yourself?"

"Yessum, ma'am."

"I mean no harm to you, but your stitching is remarkable. I've only seen this kind of work in some of the finest dress shops in Paris. If you don't mind, what is your name?"

"Hattie, ma'am. Itz Hattie, ma'am," the gal replied, easing the hem of her dress from Penny's grasp in order to slightly lift her dress in a timid curtsy. The gesture exposed petite, gray legs, which were stuck in a pair of dingy, dirt-covered, well-worn boots that appeared to be older than she was. Her speech was a bit clearer than most other Negroes that lived around those parts.

With a light yet friendly smile, Penny continued, "Well, Hattie, my name is Penny, and I noticed you sitting over here sewing…" Penny stopped in amazement as she studied and admired the cross-stitches in the dress. Every seam was lined up perfectly; the hem Hattie had so diligently sewn into the fabric was ideal in every way. "I could use some help in my dress shop, and, well, I was wondering if you would come and work for me."

"Yessum, ma'am."

"Well, is that a 'yes' or a 'no'?"

"Yessum, ma'am."

"You would like to do it?"

"Yessum, miss, I comes and werks fo'ya."

It took a while for Penny to get used to a Negro's place because she always tried to treat everybody the same. Society wasn't going to let her do that; even though they were living in the North.

❊❊❊

Within the city, many families had servants, stopping short of actually calling them slaves. They mainly worked in and around the house and looked after the children. When the servants arrived in the mornings from their own tiny quarters somewhere on the outskirts of town, they had a list of chores to be completed before the end of the day. Should those chores not be completed, the day extended into the night until everything was done. Sometimes, instead of being paid with money, they were given clothes, food, and, on occasion, they got a place to live.

Penny soon found out that Quincy and Hattie were really husband and wife. Every day they walked five miles together, coming and going, from the edge of town. No one was really sure where the two had come from, and no one ever asked. Over the months, they became indebted to the Fews for their hospitality and generosity.

One evening, as Hattie and Quincy were preparing to leave for the night, Ambrose announced that his uncle was giving him land in Georgia and that he and the family would almost immediately be moving to Augusta. Ambrose did not have much money; therefore, having the land would provide new prospects for his family. "Quincy," Ambrose started. "I would like for you and Hattie to come with us. You have been good to this family, and it seems only fair we return the favor." Ambrose was far from a selfish man and did good for others because he always expected it to come back to him.

The couple stood speechless for a moment and seemed to be unsure of what was being asked of them. "Suh?" Quincy asked at a complete loss.

Almost yelling as if Quincy were deaf, Ambrose repeated his statement, "We want you to come to Georgia with us, so you can get a fresh start. Litton is a young man now and needs to learn some responsibility. There's enough land out there for him to start a family, and I was thinking maybe you and Hattie might want to have one of your own, too." Ambrose always approached things as if he were standing before the royal court. "I know you probably wondering how you going to get along down there, considering the environment and all, but we are going to protect you and promise to not let anybody hurt you."

"Yessuh. I'se unda-stand, suh, but me and mah wife us…"

Over the years, Ambrose had been around enough White men to learn their ways, which included the power of Negro manipulation when there was something he wanted, and Quincy was aware of that. Hearing the hesitation, Ambrose sweetened the deal. "I tell you what, Quincy. You and Hattie can have your own house, and we will even give you a bit of land for you to farm on. How does that sound to you?"

His eyes dancing from corner to corner and floorboard to floorboard, Quincy began to stammer through his words; for it was something he did when he felt confused and threatened. "S-s-s-suh, if I'se c-c-c-could haf s-s-sum time t-t-t-to thank 'bout it. Us iz fine up hare in d-d-de norf, suh."

With his face turning slightly red and a frown settling between his eyes, Ambrose said matter-of-factly, "That is fine, Quincy. We will just take Hattie with us, so she can continue to help out my wife with her sewing and such. She is still good for breeding and will make me a good bit of money down there on my plantation."

Hattie stood, clenching her husband's hand with her eyes staring holes in the wooden floor. Biting her lip until tiny drips of blood trickled from the corners of her mouth, Hattie turned and buried her face into her husband's sleeve, sobbing. She trusted Penny, but, from the very first day she started working in the dress shop, she knew Ambrose, even though he was from London, was like the rest of the White men she had known. Soon after the start of her work with Penny, her responsibilities as Penny's assistant quickly transformed into chores for the entire family. Initially upon morning arrival, Hattie would color code dress orders so that Penny would know which ones were to receive top priority. Then it would be off to the general store for the necessary threads, buttons, and zippers. By the time she returned, Penny would have laid out the many bolts of fabric for her to begin cutting. After the cutting was done, Hattie would assist with the stitching until the dress was complete.

Whenever customers stopped in, it was Penny who greeted them at the door with the usual pleasantries, but Hattie was the one who made sure every seam followed every curve to a tee right down to the way the perfected lines draped around their hoops.

One afternoon when Penny could not tear herself away from a wedding gown she had been working on, she told Hattie what to cook and asked her to prepare it and then take Ambrose his lunch. Thinking nothing of the request, Hattie made Ambrose's favorites as requested; a sandwich of potatoes and cured ham. However, when she sat the food in front of him, he chastised her for bringing him pig when he had distinctly asked for a bowl of soup.

"Do you not know how to follow orders, Hattie?" he asked firmly as he looked at her over his spectacles. He towered above everybody he came in contact with, standing over six feet tall. When he sat in his chairs, he had to almost fold his legs underneath him to be able to sit at the table or his writing desk. With light reddish-brown hair, Ambrose's blue eyes made him look like the other White men in Baltimore. The only thing that separated him from the natives was his English brogue that occasionally disappeared when he was speaking to his regulars or when he was giving orders to Quincy. Every so often Ambrose's dialect reminded Hattie of where she came from, a place where she never planned to return.

"Yessuh, I does, suh."

Pushing the plate away, Ambrose leaned back in his chair, intertwining his fingers. He began tapping the tips of his thumbs together as put his eyes on the imprints of Hattie's breasts against her dress. "Why don't you come closer to me so I can explain to you what I expect for my lunch?"

During that time, there was no such thing as "no" when it came to doing what a White man said. "Yessuh," she replied, walking slowly over to where Ambrose was sitting. She stopped just short of his arms-reach.

"Are you scared, gal? I'm not going to hurt you. I only want to talk."

Hattie knew Ambrose was lying, but, out of her respect for what Penny expected of her when it came to following orders, she moved closer to him. "Yessuh," she said.

Standing close enough to land a wad of spit directly in his eyeball, Hattie folded her arms over her chest, looked up toward the sky to the Lord, and then closed her eyes. A few seconds later, she, trembling like a leaf on the magnolia tree that stood in the meadow where she first met Quincy, felt Ambrose's hands pull her hands from her chest. Her resistance was not strong enough to protect her from his quick grasps. Writhing in agony and embarrassment, she held her tears until the wells of her eyes were full. They poured from her like the river that she and Quincy traveled north to escape the horrors of Georgia.

Soon she felt Ambrose's large palms embrace her bosom. Abandoning her struggle, she relaxed herself against his desk and let him begin to have his way with her.

He rose from his chair and slid it toward the wall. Pressing himself between her legs, Ambrose's breathing became quicker and heavier as he pushed his body against hers. Hattie, feeling his manhood stuck up against her stomach, silently prayed for a savior while reluctantly allowing herself to be satisfied. Before she knew it, her hands clutched the desk on both sides of her as he began to raise her dress to reach what was beneath. Just as he had loosened his belt buckle and put his fingertips on the top of the zipper, he heard the bells from the front door jingle, but he could not and would not stop what he had begun. He heard the door close but ignored the fast-approaching foot-steps that halted at the doorway to his office.

"Suh?"

Hattie's eyes popped open to the stunned tone of her hus-band's voice. She quickly dropped the hem of her dress and ran past Quincy, out the door and down the street. Ambrose, not the least bit embarrassed, adjusted himself and fastened his belt buckle.

"Quincy, we got to teach you how to knock when you walk into a room. You never know what you might walk into."

Ambrose slowly pulled his chair back up to the desk, refusing to hazard a glance in Quincy's direction.

"Y-y-yessuh." Quincy blinked. He had been violated, yet again. Standing there with feet seemingly glued to the floor, he con-templated whether or not running away—again—would change anything.

2

D inner was eaten in silence as Hattie and Quincy asked and answered questions within themselves. Hattie was unsure about how to explain what had happened earlier, and Quincy wasn't sure how to explain what he had seen. They had come to Baltimore from Savannah, Georgia to escape death, and Quincy said he would die first before going back there. It had taken him years to regain his dignity, and now, with Ambrose proving he was like the rest, he was watching himself lose it again. While he wanted to believe none of what he had seen was Hattie's fault, he did not see her try-ing to fight off the man. Quincy wanted to believe that his love for Hattie would keep him from thinking she had been about to give in to human nature, and not forcefulness, that afternoon.

"You wus lettin' him tetch ya," he said softly as he slowly pushed a corn cake into his mouth. "You won't tryin' to fight 'em."

Sitting at the table, staring at her food, Hattie swallowed hard as if she were trying to remove a rock lodged in her throat, and then said, "Wut I'se s'pose to do, Quincy? He come at me and I do the only thang I knowed to do."

"It ain't s'pose to be lak dat up norf. De massas, dey s'pose to be betta than dat," Quincy said disgustedly. Highly disappointed in Ambrose's actions, he continued, "He jes lak de res uh dem."

"Dey's gon be de same no matta whar we go," Hattie assured him. "I knowed one thang, tho. Us cain't go back to Joe-jee."

"Wut chos us got, Hattie?"

"Us kin run."

"Te whar? Us ain't got no whars else te go," Quincy said, slamming his hand against the table. "Massa knowed I'se ain't gon let ya leave widout me. He knowed dat."

"Quincy, you knowed dey gon kill ya if dey find ya down dere, an dey might as well take me on wid ya cus I'se ain't gon be no use to a soul widout ya."

Quincy got up from the table and walked over to where Hattie sat. Standing over her, he embraced her shoulders and pressed her back into his body. "I'se gon be fine, Hattie. I'se tole ya I'se always protek ya. Us gon be alright. Us gon go wid massa if-n he say so. He seh he gon protek us," he said. "He kin protek us from de uh-ders."

Hattie did not trust that. Just like Ambrose had made it a point to remind Quincy he could take her against her will if he wanted, she knew Ambrose, or some other White man, would betray them if it ever came down to it.

❊❊❊

By the way Massa Theron Gray ran his plantation, Grayson Manor, it was hard to tell there had ever been a ban on slavery in Savannah. With nearly a third of the colony's people being slaves, most every one of them belonged, or used to belong to Massa Gray or somebody in his family. No one was really sure what went on with that family to make them stop looking for and caring after one of their own, but none of them had anything to do with Massa Gray. They would see him on the square in town and turn their heads when they saw him coming, and his slaves were not treated any better. When they found out a nigger was belonging to him, they were extra nasty by spitting on them and beating them in the streets.

Marriages on the plantation were forbidden because they interfered with work and loyalty to Massa Gray. The cabins were made of logs, and each cabin was big enough to hold two families; if necessary. The spaces between the logs were filled with mud and straw, rarely keeping the wind and rain from entering. There was no glass in the windows—only shutters that were rarely closed, for keeping out the glory of God was simply unheard of. Although the floors were made of dirt, many of the slaves made the best of their homes and kept them well-maintained. All of the women and children lived on one side of the quarters, and the men lived on the other. One would think that it would be strange to prevent breeding and deny oneself the chance to make money, but, for Massa Gray, there was more to life than money. When he needed more help, he relied on a slave trader to go to the auctions near the port of Savannah and bring him back some good help. Sometimes it was really hard to tell where he got those niggers from because they all looked different, and had many stories inside them to tell about their people. Late at night, after the lights went out in the main house, they sat around the fire and talked about where they came from and all the places they had been to, before sailing to the states. For many of them, their entire families had been torn apart or had died while on the cargo ships. Day after day, bodies were thrown from the boats—some of them were still holding on to their lives, and others had given up the day they were put in chains.

Massa Gray did not have any children, and not once in his years had he been married. He was a fine man who looked straight through you with his cold, light-brown eyes that were empty of any emotion and exposed a man with no soul. His sandy, brown hair was thin but curly, and when he sweated, his curls were matted to his pea-sized head. Because he never lifted a finger to do a thing, he was fleshy with pockets of fat under his neck and beneath his stomach. When he whipped you, that pocket of meat beneath his chin snapped whenever the whip cracked. He struck until he got tired, and if you died before he finished, then so be it. No one was ever able to mourn. The dead were drug off to the pasture and burned in a bonfire. Massa Gray refused to waste his land on graves for slaves.

"Those holes in the ground can be used for planting—not wasted on domesticated animals. A dead nigger can't make nobody no money, but a cabbage patch sure can," he always said.

Not many folks ever came to visit Grayson Manor. On occasion, a few of the other planters came by to talk about the weather and things like that, but they did not stay very long. The only person that visited regularly was an acquaintance by the name of Silas Strong—the slave trader. It was usually around supper time when he came, but no one was sure when he left.

One evening while Quincy was sitting around the fireplace with some of the others, they spotted Silas riding in on his horse. But before he got off, he trotted over to where they were gathered. As the fire crackled, each of the men sat motionless. William, a boy of about sixteen whose twin brother had run off one night and was never seen again, stared into the flames; even though he wanted so much to ask Silas where his brother was. The last time anybody had seen him, he was with Silas. Instead, he focused on the fire. Vincent, who had lost his left eye when Massa Gray got upset with him for not putting the right amount of coals in a fire and stuck him in the eye with a hot poker, put his attention on a cricket whose crooning joined into the popping of the burning wood. Quincy kept it easy and lowered his head as Silas gently paraded behind them.

"You darkies sho' is quiet. When I rode up, I could hear you laughin' clear back down to the edge of the road," Silas said. "What is it y'all talkin' about?"

No one said a word at first. Then Vincent spoke up, "Us wus jes foolin' 'rown, Massa. Dets all us wus doin'."

"Does Master Gray know y'all out here without nothin' to do? I mean, it's plenty to be done this time of night. Ain't that right, William?" Silas jumped off his horse into the dirt—dust bellowing up to his braces—and pulled some oats out of his satchel. First he tossed a handful in the fire, and then he started feeding the rest to his horse.

"Yessuh," William responded quietly, still gazing into the fire.

Tossing one of the oats into the air and catching it with his open mouth, Silas kept his eye on Quincy but continued to direct his questions at William. His looks were wicked and sinful. "Heard anythin' from that brother of yours, William?"

"No, suh. I ain't." By now, sweat beads were popping off William's forehead like hot kernels of corn.

"Well, that's too bad. He was a good nigger." Silas walked with his horse until he got behind Quincy. "Boy, stand up," he said, leaning over from behind. "Let me take a look at you. I been talkin' to Theron about you comin' over to my place to take care of a few things." Quincy didn't move. He didn't like Silas and was willing to take whatever punishment he had to in order to prove his point. "Nigger, I know you ain't hard of hearin' 'cause I see you runnin' up behind that wench Hattie when she calls for you." Quincy still didn't move. "Okay, I see you want to be a hard ass."

When he saw that Quincy wasn't going to move, Silas started rustling with his horse until the ass of the horse was right over Quincy's head. Fortunately, the horse was gentle, but that was not what Quincy should have been counting on. "You know, boy, I came out here lookin' for no trouble, but I guess that when you go to lookin' for shit, you eventually step in it." He laughed. "What you think, boy?" Then all of them heard the horse grunt and saw him unleash his business onto Quincy's shoulders. "Well, guess it's time for me to get on up to the house." Silas mounted his horse, galloping back up the path to where Massa was standing outside waiting.

William finally looked up and saw Quincy sitting there, petrified, with the horse mess still dropping from his body. "I hear he a sissy and so is Massa."

At first no one knew what to say, but, as the night hurried on, Vincent spoke first. "Yeh, dey say him and Massa be in der doin' thangs God neva meant for mens te do. Say Massa be in der ben ova de side uh de bed wit Massa Silas right up 'hind 'em. U kin heer dem sum-times late in de night."

"I heared dat, too," William said. "Seh dey gat a posse uh dem dat go 'rown skerrin' the slaves at night. I'se believe dat wut happ'n te my brudda."

"Wut? Dat Massa Silas got te 'um?"

"Yeah, but ain't no need'n talkin' 'bout it. Ye knowed dey

prolly kilt 'em. Des rott-n like dat." William started throwing dirt on the fire, signaling it was time to turn in for the night. As the orange faded from the ashes, they watched Quincy work to get himself cleaned off, but offered no assistance.

✪✪✪

Walking down to the river at night was something most of the slaves never did, let alone walking down there by themselves. While it was always beautiful to see the moon sitting up there against the blue-black sky and hear the crickets singing their songs, it could quickly become the longest walk anybody could ever take. Quincy had asked Vincent to take the walk with him, but Vincent insisted he was tired and needed to go to bed. The others had disappeared shortly after Silas had left.

As he walked along the red clay sodden from an earlier rain, Quincy heard the owls and the night creatures carrying on as they normally did. The river was about a mile from the quarters, and the closer Quincy got to the rushing water, the further away it seemed. Step by barefoot step, he watched his large footprints squish into the earth, which made him remember the day he had met Hattie. She was sitting in the middle of the yard next to a Magnolia tree with Eunice playing in the mud, and she was about six years old at the time. The two of them were sitting knee deep in a pile of wet earth, making and selling mud pies.

"Ya want one uh dees?" she asked. "Dey cost uh nickel but Ise givs it t'ya fa free."

Quincy was ten and had been working in the fields with his father for years. Hattie was only old enough to fetch things for

Massa Gray; he did not have much for the younger niggers to do. Smiling with his crooked yellow-stained teeth gleaming in the sunshine, Quincy reached for the mud pie and said, "Well, th-th-th-thank ya. I'se gonna eat it all up, too!"

From that moment on, Quincy and Hattie played together when time would let them, and, as she grew older, Hattie felt a sense of protection with him. By the time Quincy was seventeen, he was a big man with round, chipped golden brown muscles from the top of his shoulders to the bottom of his thighs. Hattie had seen thirteen birthdays, and, despite their difference in age and her massa's rules about relations in the quarters, she had promised herself to Quincy.

The second she set her eyes on Quincy, she knew he would have her heart forever. Her friends often teased her about her glassy stares when she spoke his name. She had taught herself to make simple stitches in fabric by watching Eunice's grandmother make Massa Gray's shirts. Daily, Hattie would ask for the scraps so she could practice and perhaps one day help make Massa Gray's clothes. Before too long, she had enough scraps to make a shirt that she gave to Quincy, and, from the time she gave it to him, he wore that shirt every single day and nothing kept him from it. Whenever they were less than only a few feet from one another, Hattie memorized his scent and fixed it in her nose so she would know when he had just left a room or space she entered. With his shadow absorbing her tiny frame whenever they stood close, she became one with him, knowing he would always protect her. In their quarters, the females were supposed to do all the cooking and cleaning for the men. After they finished in the main house, they planted flowers around the bushes and up and down the path leading to the main road.

Just as the other females her age, Hattie's responsibilities were few but sometimes difficult. If she had to wheel dirt to the front yard for planting, she did it with all her might, but, within an instant, Quincy would appear. If she had to go out back and kill a chicken for dinner, she would get as far as picking out the chicken and taking it to the backyard. Having to step away to check the pot of boiling water, she'd return to the chicken, finding its neck already wrung and its head cut off. Once the chores of the main house were tended to, the females returned to the quarters to prepare dinner for the men who had been in the fields all day. Every night since the first day she had laid eyes on Quincy, there was a sunflower from massa's flower bed laying atop the single blanket on which she slept. She knew that whenever that stopped, Quincy's love for her was gone, or he was dead.

❂❂❂

The night marched on to the rhythm of Quincy's footsteps, and the sound of the water had gotten louder. Quincy knew it would take a while, if ever, to get the odor out of his skin, and then next he was going to have to wash his clothes. As he approached the river, he could smell the muscadine patches that enveloped the trees alongside the banks. Taking great care in where he stepped because cotton mouths lingered around the brushes for the nectar of the muscadines, Quincy began to disrobe, piece by piece, and then entered the water, taking his clothes with him.

In one deep breath, Quincy submerged himself, cleansing his body and his clothes in the muddied waters. When he came to the surface and was preparing to step back onto the bank, he noticed an uneasy calm surrounding him. The river was still as it appeared flat against the moonlight. There were no crickets, no owls, not one sound coming from the nature around him. Quickly, Quincy twisted the water from his pants and put on his shirt, still dripping with water. Hurriedly passing through the muscadine patches and mashing the sugary juices between his toes, he stopped just beyond the edge of the brush, hearing what he thought to be a horse trying to catch its breath. In the darkness and unsure about which way to turn, Quincy tried desperately to listen for the rippling of the river, but he couldn't hear it. He did, however, hear the whinny of a horse and its anger with being held back. As his heart began to race, and realizing that he was not alone, Quincy started running and thought to himself to never look back. The only thing he wanted to do was to get back to the quarters so he could see Hattie. *CRACK!* The blow to his skull made him fall to the ground face first.

With the earth below him saturating his tongue, Quincy's trousers were ripped from his lower body like paper exposing his backside and the miniscule curly, black hairs that covered his skin. It felt to him that each one of them was standing straight in the air as he was rammed in the rectum with another man's wooden peck. He was ordered to lie still and threatened with castration if he made a sound or tried to get away. "Don't fight me, nigger, or I'll get that winch of yours and do the same, if not worse, to her."

Quincy recognized the voice above him as that of Silas, but there was another he also recognized. Soon the other voice, that of Massa Gray who had knelt between the V-shaped contour of

Quincy's anatomy, was right in his ear, and he entered Quincy's shell with a hardened cock, causing him to tense his muscles even harder.

"That's a good nigger," he soothed. "Hold it right there."

A single tear rolled from the corner of his eye down his cheek and onto his hand that was flat beneath his face. His other hand was pinned behind him. One thrust after another, the attack went on for what seemed like forever until the walls of Quincy's bowels could not take it anymore, and he let loose like a rabbit that had gotten hold of some bad grass.

"You fucking nigger!" Massa Gray shouted. "You're going to pay for this with your life!"

Both men, with themselves still at attention, scrambled to their feet to get to their holsters they had tossed into the brush. While they tousled through the darkness, Quincy, lying there with his manhood stripped from him, braced himself to make a run for his life. Slowly raising to his feet just enough so as to not be seen, Quincy took off like a bolt of lightning, being guided by only the moonlight. Every stride he took, with bullets blasting past his head, was for the life he wanted with Hattie, but he knew would never have that at Grayson Manor.

❂❂❂

Runaways were simply considered "missing." In the company of servants, Silas, known for his sometimes barbaric antics, was asked by Massa Gray to keep a watchful eye out for those who had escaped and to deal with them accordingly if they were ever caught outside the boundaries of the plantation. Nearly everyone knew that Silas and Massa Gray had something to do with the disappearances. They had never raised a fuss about it more than a day or two. None of the women rarely, if ever, tried to leave. For the most part, they were safe and were rewarded for their obedience and loyalty. For the men, however, there was something different. While, on the surface, they had no reason to run away, there existed a reason that remained within the confines of their quarters. Most times they were singled out in front of their counterparts and subsequently taunted and humiliated to the point of self-destruction. In the case of William's twin brother, Wayne, Massa Gray and Silas had followed him into the corn fields one morning and tailed him until they had reached a section where the crows had gotten to the stalks.

"Wayne, what you go and let them birds eat up my corn for?" Massa Gray asked.

Wayne, looking around at the others in the field with him until he laid his eyes upon his brother, answered, "Suh, I ain't knowed dees burds wus comin' out heer lak dis. I'se kin git a scahrcrow uh sumthin' te make dem goes away."

Silas walked over to Wayne and grabbed him by the front of his shirt. "Boy, why should you go through all that when you got a scarecrow already out here?"

"Suh?" Wayne asked baffled.

Then Silas snatched off Wayne's shirt and slammed it to the ground. "We got you!" He cackled, studying Wayne's bare chest. Silas got closer to Wayne and began making circles with his fingertips. "You is all we need out here. You black, you ugly, and I'm pretty sho' you can scare away a bunch of little bitty ol' birds."

Shirtless, Wayne stood there waiting for Massa Gray to say something, but no words ever came. "Massa Silas, suh, wuh you want me te do, suh?"

As Silas stood there with his hazel-green eyes piercing through the sweaty flesh of William's twin brother, he replied, "I want you to get up there on that there pole and scare them crows off your master's crops."

"Yessuh," Wayne offered silently and proceeded to climb up the pole to take his stand.

Laughing out loud and looking to Massa Gray for approval, Silas called out, "You sho' is a dumb nigger."

Wayne looked confused as he stepped back onto the ground. "Iz der sumthin' 'rong, suh?"

"Well, hell, yes, somethin's wrong. You ain't no damn good to the them crows with your pants on. You gotta get up there on that pole and show them birds how ugly you is. I want you to take your pants off and get on up there and scare them birds away."

Under the apologetic eyes of the other field hands, Wayne removed his pants and got up on the pole and sat perched in the sun until his skin and the bird droppings melted into one. Later in the night, Wayne took a walk down to the river, and a few minutes later Silas left the house going in the same direction. Wayne was never seen again.

❂❂❂

A whole day had gone by, and Hattie had not seen Quincy. Although she did not mind doing the chores without his assistance, she thought perhaps Quincy was too busy to help her at different times throughout the day. Massa Gray was good for hiring out some of the men to work for others, and they may be gone for days at a time. Even then, though, Quincy made his way back to the quarters to put a sunflower on Hattie's blanket. When she got home that night, there was no flower waiting for her.

After the lights went out in the main house, that's when the men and women would sneak out of their cabins and meet around a small fire at the back of quarters; closest to the edge of the woods. Those that had eyes for each other sat and held hands until the sun had started to brighten the sky. Others who had gone beyond hand-holding disappeared into the trees and did what came naturally to them. On the few occasions that a wench ended up with child, Massa Gray sold her at the auction. To punish her for disobeying him, he had Silas cut a deal with the new owner by refunding his money and paying him back twice what he had paid, if he gave the baby back to Massa Gray when it was born. And that is exactly how Hattie ended up on the plantation.

Hattie looked out her back door and saw the others getting on and laughing around the fire but didn't see Quincy. She contemplated going out to ask where he was, but she did not want to spoil the evening for the others. Taking a seat in a chair next to the table where she kept an arrangement of sunflowers, Hattie released a waterfall from her eyes. She knew she had done nothing to make Quincy stop loving her; therefore, she had no choice but to think otherwise. Then, as she buried her head into her folded arms on the table, there was a soft knock at the door.

Wiping away her tears and drying her hands against her gingham dress, Hattie opened the door and saw Vincent, with Eunice by his side, standing before her with his head hung low. "Uh, Miss Hattie, uh, how ye dis evenin'?"

Hattie replied calmly, "I'se gettin' long fine, Vincent. Wut kin I do fa ye?"

"Miss Hattie, me and the fellas out der knowed 'bout you and

Quancy," he responded. "Us knowed he quite fond uh ya. Dat's why sumbody needed te come tell ya 'bout last night."

"Please, c'mon in. Tells me er'ythang."

By the time Vincent finished telling her all that had happened, Hattie had no life left in her and fell into his arms, continuing to weep uncontrollably.

Eunice helped take Hattie from Vincent's arms. "I gots hur. Gone bak outside fo' ya gits ketched in here wid us." Until Hattie started falling asleep, Eunice sat with her and wiped her tears as they flowed into her lap. "Miss Hattie, I'ma get on home unlessen ya needs me te stay here wid ya."

Her eyes wet as rain puddles, she told Eunice to go on home so she could spend some time talking with Jesus. A short time later, there was another knock at the door, and Hattie thought maybe Eunice had decided to come back to check on her. But when she opened the door, no one was there. Standing in the door's threshold, a gentle wind passed by, and with it was the scent of Quincy. Hattie closed the door and headed toward the corner where she slept, but noticed the back door was slightly open. She got up and closed it, peeping through the crack to see if someone had tried to get in. With the flames of a nearby candle flickering against the wooden floor, her eyes fell upon the top of the pile of straw where she slept. Against her blanket was a sunflower. When she leaned over to pick it up, her senses detected an odor enhanced by the scent of her man. "Quincy?" she called out.

Emerging from the corner of the room that received the least amount of light was Quincy. "Shhhh," he directed with his finger pressed against his lips.

"But wut…"

Having returned to the site where he was attacked to get his pants, Quincy was clothed, but his shirt and pants were in shreds. "I'se need ya te get ya thangs real quick, Hattie, and comes on wid me."

Without hesitation, Hattie grabbed her blanket and her flowers. "I'se ready." Disappearing into the night, the two runaways left their troubles behind and sought freedom.

❋❋❋

The next morning it was quickly discovered that Hattie was missing since she worked in the main house from time to time, being responsible for bringing Massa Gray his breakfast. By the break of dawn, he was coming down the stairs, and, before the sun could shed light into the east side of the house, he was sitting at the table with his breakfast of eggs, bacon, and biscuits waiting for him. Ever since Hattie had been working in the house, that was the routine, but on this particular morning, there was no smell of bacon frying or biscuits baking. The minute Massa Gray got to the top of the stairs he knew something was wrong, and, instead of going to the table, he went to the barn to get his horse and headed over to see Silas.

"We got a problem, Silas. Hattie's run off," Massa Gray said as he walked toward Silas, who was about to sit down to his breakfast of eggs, grits and hoecakes.

"Well, then, you must be hungry. Have some," Silas joked, gesturing for his servant, Nan, to fix Massa Gray a plate. Checking to see if Nan was out of sight, he continued. "I know you ain't surprised. We was shootin' bullets in the dark, and you musta missed." He laughed.

"Silas, we can't afford to have that nigger out there. He could…"

"He could what? Tell? Tell who? He wouldn't live a second longer if he opened up his mouth to a White man about it, and he too shamed to tell another nigger. We ain't got nothin' to worry about."

Massa Gray sat there still looking concerned. He was spiteful and evil when he wanted to be. "We need him dead, Silas. We can't risk somebody finding out."

Silas, shoveling hot grits in his mouth with one hand, put his other hand on Massa Gray's thigh and started rubbing his hand up and down and around his cock. "Tell you what. I got an idea."

"What?"

"We can post a reward for Hattie. Now you and I both know we don't give a damn about her. Wherever we find Hattie, we find Quincy."

3

In 1799, a few years after his father passed away, William Few left Augusta for New York City and left the land to Ambrose, who had been in Richmond County for ten years. In small spots, he had begun experimenting with cotton crops and soon found himself with the respect of many Augusta businessmen. When William had first arrived in the South, he immediately began work on the home that would be passed on for generations to become. It was far from finished at his departure, and the rest of the work was left to be completed under the direction of Ambrose and Litton.

Taking nearly twelve years to complete, the big house, situated along a piece of land that sat comfortably beside the Savannah River, stood three-stories with the kitchen, dining room, parlor, sitting rooms, and library on the first floor. Penny had sewn fancy coverings for the windows and furniture, selecting only the finest European fabrics money could buy. Two of the sitting rooms were adorned with artwork and sculptures Ambrose had collected over the years. Once a month, Ambrose and Quincy traveled to Charleston to meet the cargo ships that brought in fine furnishings from England. Nearly every piece of furniture in the house was made of imported mahogany and upholstered in English paisley-printed tapestry.

On the second floor, there were four bedrooms for family members and guests. Each room's décor was luxurious with bedspreads, curtains, and pillows made of fine, imported cottons. Silk, hard to find due to the decrease in its manufacture, was apparent in every room. Penny had it imported from France and often made extra money by selling it to some of the other wives. The top floor was strictly for the children, with enough space for them to read, play, and sleep if they wanted to. It could only be reached by the servants' stairs at the back of the house. The grounds, with beautiful magnolia trees lining the path that led out to main road, were tended to daily and boasted gardens of roses, tulips, and sunflowers. From the main road, there was a long-winding road stretching for over a mile, and when you reached the clearing, you were at the sprawling estate of Fews Grove.

Penny quickly became the English socialite she had once been and primed June for high status among the Southern elite. From time to time, Penny adorned her acquaintances with beautiful handmade garments. It was no secret that Hattie made those things, and Penny took all the credit for it. Needless to say, it did not take long for Penny to adopt the Southern mentality she had protested for most of her life. She had two house servants, Mildred and Paul. Like the other slaves the Fews had inherited, they were treated very well and never had reason to be unhappy.

Nearing his thirties, Quincy worked as Ambrose's driver until his death in 1805. The land had been willed to Litton and June, but as she was against slavery, June met a young Quaker from New England who was visiting Augusta on business. She had grown not to want any connection to the Southern traditions her family had adopted. The incident that marred her for life was

the day she saw her grandfather whip a slave, and it tormented
her for a great portion of her early life. June felt her father had
abandoned his promise to never allow slavery to ruin his value
system, and, over the years, she saw the demise of that assurance.
At the urging of her mother, June and her husband moved to
Massachusetts. Seeing that she, too, had succumbed to the ways
of the South, Penny joined them and lived with them until her
death.

Litton had been trained by his great-uncle on how to maintain the land and how to manage the slaves he'd inherited. Under
the elder Few's control, the slaves had grown accustomed to
having no liberties about the plantation, with everyone being
treated equally. There was no such thing as different treatment
for light-skinned and dark-skinned slaves. Every shade carried
the same number of chores and the same punishment. Litton,
however, was more like his father and had very little desire to
uphold slavery and its cruelties. He considered them more as
indentured servants than slaves. Like Hattie and Quincy, they
were given small pieces of land in exchange for their service to
the family.

By 1815, the cotton crops had become very profitable for Litton,
and he was ready to become a family man. A bit older than the
other men he knew, Litton, on Christmas Day of the same year,
finally married Risella Andrews, the granddaughter of Don
Manuel de Montiano—the once governor of St. Augustine
who led the Spanish organized invasion of Georgia in 1742.
Fifteen years his junior, Risella was expecting their first and
only child within two months of their marriage. A month after
their baby girl, Annie Isabella Few, was born, Hattie gave birth
to her and Quincy's son, Josiah.

❂❂❂

A year to the day after Josiah was born, Risella sent Hattie into town to pick up some candles and cereal for the baby. Hattie carefully strolled around the store to make sure she'd gotten the right items for Risella. As she tried to reach the top shelf where the candles were, she felt Mr. Alex watching her every move. She'd been to the store many times before, but this visit was strange for her. Normally, Mr. Alex greeted her warmly because she was from the Fews' place, and he looked upon them as good people. When she had been in there before, however, Mr. Alex asked her a bunch of questions like where were her folks from and was she married. Hattie willingly answered his questions without thinking. What Hattie was not aware of was Mr. Alex had seen a poster when he was last in Savannah, and it had a very good description of Hattie on it, and then it said she was traveling with a nigger they called Quincy.

"What you want, gal?" Mr. Alex asked harshly.

Hattie, who had aged well to be in her thirties but had the hands of a sixty-year-old woman, replied, "I gots dis here candle and…"

"Git on way from here," he demanded. "Go on, git!"

Not understanding why Mr. Alex was acting in such a way, Hattie did as she was asked. She simply left out the back door. When she got outside, she went around to the front to begin her journey to the other side of town to go to another store. For whatever reason Mr. Alex had denied her service, she was forced to go home and share her experience with Risella. Across the street from Mr. Alex's store was the jail and gathered in front of it was a coalition of White men sitting on top of their horses. Amongst themselves, they were passing around papers that appeared to have the faces and images of slaves on them. The only time there was a nigger on a poster was when they were looking for him.

Eyes were on her, and she felt them burning a hole in her skin. As the men laughed at one another, she noticed one of them take a look down at the paper and then glance up at her. Quickly, Hattie covered her head with her wrap and walked in the opposite direction to begin her journey home. When she was a few feet away, she looked back and saw the gang run off in the other direction. Knowing she could not go home without Risella's request, Hattie walked as fast as she could, and in every other step or two, she ran to be able to get home before the sun began to set. The last thing she needed was to have a slave catcher get a good glimpse of her because she knew somebody, somewhere, was looking for them.

❂❂❂

Silas Strong, over the years, maintained his reputation for being brutal with captured runaways. He was still in the slave-trading business, but it was his dealings with the runaways in which he took the most pride. In his earlier days, he was gentler, if you call what he and Massa Gray had done to Quincy gentle. Often times, he convinced the owners to give him the go-ahead to go on and kill the niggers if he caught them. So far, he had found mostly all of the slaves he was hired to capture, and, rightfully so, he killed almost every one of them except for Quincy. He did not want anyone to know that he had failed, so what he did was up the ante for Hattie, doubling the reward. Years had gone by, but Silas Strong refused to be outdone by two niggers. Riding fiercely through the woods at a speed only seen by lightning, Silas, Massa Gray, and the rest of them came up on the Few place like thunder.

"Litton Few, come on out here, son," Silas's angry voice requested.

Litton, holding Annie close to his chest while her mother bathed, peeped out the front window and was astonished to see the gang standing outside his house. He passed the baby to a waiting servant and opened the door. "Can I help you, sir?"

Sitting up high in the saddle, the man answered without exchanging any pleasantries. "My name is Silas Strong, and I'm a slave catcher from Savannah. I hear you keeping one of my runaway niggers out here."

"Sir," Litton offered, "I assure you we don't have any runaways around this place. These servants were my father's and he…"

Silas reached into his pocket and pulled out a piece of folded paper. "Read that and tell me if you don't have a slave here that fits that description," he demanded, shoving the paper at Litton.

"Petite and thin, about thirty to forty years old, speaks decent English, has no marks on her body, sews and is good at spinning silk—whoever takes her up will be rewarded. She answers to the name of Hattie and may be traveling with a dangerous nigger answering to Quincy," Litton read aloud. There had to have been a mistake. "Sir, I'm sorry, but I can't help you. We don't have a slave around here by that name."

Silas dismounted his horse and walked up to Litton until they were square in the face. "You gotta mighty fine place here, son. Heard your pa did pretty good for himself."

Proudly, Litton answered, "Well, thank you. We do alright around here. We…"

Without warning, Silas grabbed Litton by the arms, squeezing them with his fingertips and piercing into his skin. "Look here, you nigger lover. I will burn this place down to the ground, with everybody in it. That means you, your crops, and your family," he snarled.

Litton knew Hattie had gone off to the store and it would be almost dark before she got back. Just as he was about to respond, Risella came to the door. "Litton, honey, is everything alright?"

"Go back in the house, Risella. I'll be there in a minute." He took two steps back from Silas, saying as he looked back toward his house, "They are not here, but I can tell you where they are. Wait here."

While Silas was no fool, he gave Litton the benefit of the doubt. "You got two minutes, son."

"Okay, thank you." Litton walked hurriedly up the steps and into the house where he found Risella waiting by the door with Annie in her arms. "Risella, I need you to go down to Hattie and Quincy's place to get Josiah and bring him back here. Quincy's there with him. Send him to the barn and tell him to wait there until he hears from me."

"Oh, my goodness, Litton. What's going on?"

"Just do as I say. Go out the back door and make sure no one sees you."

"Okay." Risella gave Annie to the waiting servant and headed toward the back door.

Litton knew no one would stop his wife, but he unfortunately did not know Silas. He returned to the window and saw Silas anxiously waiting. He went back outside. "Uh, Mr. Strong?" Litton offered, "Hattie's out running an errand for my wife, and, uh, Quincy, he's on his way up here."

Silas only wanted Quincy and really could not have cared less about Hattie. "I thought you'd do the right thing."

He and the others had patiently waited for nearly half an hour, but there was still no Quincy. Litton was sitting on the porch, waiting to hear the back door open.

"Now, son, I might be a fool sometimes, but I ain't no ol' fool," Silas said, leaning against the stair rail to the porch. "I sho' hope you ain't…"

Litton heard the back door slam. "Excuse me, Mr. Strong. I'll be right back."

Silas gestured for one of his men to go around to the back of the house to stand watch. After Quincy and Hattie had run away, Silas made it his business to make sure he never stopped until he found them. He had all but given up, until the day he received a message from Mr. Alex. Earlier in the day, when Hattie had left the store, Silas was hiding behind a tree, waiting to see if Mr. Alex had been right in his identification. There was a seven hundred dollar price on Hattie, or her whereabouts. As soon as she exited through the back of the store, Massa Gray had entered the front door to pay Mr. Alex the reward.

Risella arrived back at the house with Josiah covered in a blanket and took him upstairs to the third floor. Litton was waiting for her at the bottom of the stairs when she was finished. "What are you doing?" Risella asked tearfully.

"I'm saving our lives. Do you realize they will kill us, if I don't give them Quincy?"

Risella, who had a soft spot for Hattie and Quincy, answered, "This will kill Hattie, and you know that. I can't believe you did this. Of all the heartless things a White man could do, you betray the man who helped raise you, who helped build this house, and who…"

Hesitantly, Litton replied, wiping his wet brow with the handkerchief he kept in his pants' pocket. "I know, but we can protect Hattie. I can't do anything for Quincy now."

As he stepped back onto the porch, Litton knew he would have trouble living with what he was about to do, but he refused to lose everything for a nigger. Ambrose, taught by an uncle, had instilled in his son that there were limits to their relationships with slaves, and imminent death was one of them. Litton could instantly tell Silas was a man of his word. "He's in the barn, but, like I said, Hattie's not here."

Mounting his horse, Silas chuckled snidely. "Can't no wench do nothin' for me. It's him I want."

✸✸✸

Dusk began to descend, and the barn had fallen still. Litton had requested one of the servants to release the horses and cows into the pasture. After waiting hours for Litton, Quincy rested against a pile of hay and stole a few hours of sleep. As the whippoorwills began their evening tributes, he dreamed of Hattie and the life they had built together, and the love he had for his son. He was eager to watch his son grow into a good man and hoped to be around when Josiah found someone to make him as happy as Hattie had made him. Awakened by the whinny of an approaching horse thought to be that of Litton's, Quincy tried to get up but found his arms and legs tied to stakes that had been driven into the ground. He was gagged with a shirt Hattie had made for him. Nude, he pulled and yanked, but the restraints were tight.

"Boy, you ain't goin' nowhere, so you might as well stop fussin'," Massa Gray said as he struck a match to light a torch that completely illuminated the barn. "And don't be looking for Litton to come for you 'cause he was the one that helped me out a little and sent for you."

Quincy had thought that he could trust Litton. He was not as harsh as his father and appeared genuine in his feelings and actions. With his fate looking upon him like the devil about to prey on unsuspecting soul, he was grateful Miss Risella had come for Josiah. The only thing he wanted now was to see Hattie one last time while he could still see the light of day, but he knew that would never happen. He prayed for God to have mercy on his soul as he gave up the desire to fight. Quincy lifted his head from the floor of the barn to see Massa Gray, Silas, and a man that went by the name of Will Brown encircling him. Each of them was naked, their cocks erect, as drips from early eruptions trickled to the ground.

"Boy, I hope you didn't think we were going to let you run off with one of my niggers and get away with it." Quincy just lay there. "We looked high and low for you until we gave up and called upon the Lord to bring you back to us, and I be damned if we ain't all finally back together again. The Lord is good," Massa Gray testified.

Silas walked over to Quincy and started kissing him on his chest until he reached the line where his bush began. "You know how long I been waitin' to taste this?" he asked. Silas glided his hands across Quincy's cock, anticipating nature sending blood rushing through it.

Awaiting the torturous stripping away of his dignity, Quincy lay there, shaking his head in rejection.

As he watched Quincy rise, Will walked over to Massa Gray and began kissing him intensely. Returning the affections, Massa Gray took hold of Will's pecker and touched it with his and then, releasing his grip on Will's lips, he turned him around and forced himself into him. All the while they both had their eyes on Quincy, who was now fully stiff. His eyes bulged from their sockets as he tried to fight it, but he could not win. A black hood was forced over his head, shielding him from the gradual deterioration and degradation of the last minutes of his life. Massa Gray walked over to where his clothes were strewn and pulled a hunting knife from the pile. Grasping Quincy at the point where God had made him a man, in one swift swing, Massa Gray fulfilled the promise he had made several years earlier.

❂❂❂

Throughout the night, Litton tossed and turned in bed wondering what misfortune had come to the servant that had helped raise him. While Ambrose worked, it was Quincy who had taught Litton how to mount and ride a horse, whittle pieces of wood into daggers, and catch fireflies in the summertime. It was Quincy who laid the last bricks on the big house. Litton admired the love Quincy had for Hattie and modeled his own affections for Risella after him. On the day Josiah was born, Litton gave the new parents a silk blanket his mother had made some years before. In some ways, Litton felt betrayed because he could not believe that Quincy and Hattie would put the lives of everyone on the plantation at risk by hiding out there, if they were indeed runaways.

"Risella?" he asked, tapping his wife on the shoulder as she slept. "Are you asleep?"

"Not really, dear," she responded, stretching and yawning simultaneously. Risella, who was of medium build with curly locks of jet-black hair and blue eyes, had kept close to Hattie during her pregnancy, and, often times, they shared things between one another that had been for no one else to ever hear. "What's wrong?"

Litton, dressed in a cotton nightgown given to him by his mother, sat up in the bed and rested his head against the wooden headboard Quincy had made for him. "What I did earlier was a terrible thing, and I don't know if I can live with myself for that. It's like, in a way, I was thinking like the compassionate human being my parents raised me to be, and then, in another way, I was thinking like some of these Southern monsters who have no compassion for human life. I didn't have any other choice. They were going to kill us, and I know they would not have stopped until they did."

Risella was part Spanish, and the two of them had met as passersby while visiting in town. Spaniards were rarely, if ever, seen in Augusta, and Litton was in awe of her beauty. Until she arrived there, she'd never heard of one man owning another, and, when she found out that Litton's family had slaves, she, feisty but with a beauty envied by many, set ground rules from the very beginning. The slaves were not to be mistreated in any way, and the family would not be in the business of slave breeding or slave trading. To Risella, they were extensions of the family, and, when she could get away with it, she treated them that way. Litton, however, explained how it was that he had slaves in the first place and that he never had an intention of buying any of his own. To him, they were all servants who worked for their keep.

"I need to tell you something, and you can't be angry with me for keeping it from you."

"Okay, what is it?"

Rolling over on her side so she could face her husband in the darkness, she said, "I knew they were runaways. Hattie told me a long time ago."

Litton felt his way through the dark to find the lantern but realized it might be best to leave it off. "What do you mean?"

"When they met your parents, they had only been in Baltimore for a little while and were in need of work. They didn't want to return to Georgia, but your father gave them no choice."

Recalling the day his family left Baltimore, Litton confessed, "I do remember that. Everyone but Hattie and Quincy were happy about the new opportunity."

Risella added, "I can understand you being upset by what you did, but remember, you did save that baby of theirs that's sleeping right downstairs, and you saved Hattie. Letting them stay here tonight was kind of you."

"I guess you're right. I saved his family, and that's what he would've wanted. What did you tell Hattie when she came back?"

Adjusting herself to lie on her back, Risella said hesitantly, "I told her they needed to stay with us tonight while Quincy was off doing some work down the way. I didn't know what else to say."

Litton sighed and got up from the bed to look out the window; to see if there was any movement in the barn. He wondered if they had gone ahead and taken Quincy with them. "I'm going to go out there to check on things," he said, turning from the window.

❂❂❂

Morning came to find Litton kneeling next to Quincy, who

was now lying in a puddle of his own blood, clinging to life. Litton had sent for Risella so she could fetch Hattie, and he had taken the time to remove the shirt stuffed in Quincy's mouth and cover him with a piece of burlap he had found in the back of the barn. Ever since he'd turned to walk away from Silas and his gang, Litton had been apologizing to himself, to Quincy, and to God.

Eyes fixed on the barn door, Quincy, with only a few breaths left in him, waited for Hattie, and when he saw her silhouette standing in the sunlight, a tear rolled down his cheek. Taking tiny, nervous steps at first, Hattie rubbed her hands viciously against her dress as her face became distorted at the sight of her husband. Throwing her face into her hands, the closer she got to him, her petite frame trembled until she fell upon him, sobbing as the blood soaked into her dress.

"Take me, Lawd! Take me," she pleaded. "Itz my fawt. I brangs dem right te 'em. Lawd, I brangs dem right te 'em."

Quincy, as his gaze became more and more faint, showed Hattie the bright yellow-stained teeth he had flashed at her on the day they met.

Hattie took his hand into hers and pressed it to her cheek as a steady flow of tears streamed. "We gone be aw'right, we gone be aw'right," she said, kissing the back of his hand.

Too weak to speak, he couldn't get the words out to say good-bye to her, so his heart, his eyes, and that smile of his did it for him.

4

In their old age, Silas and Massa Gray did little to conceal their relationship, and after a while, Silas moved right on in. At sunrise, they could be found riding through the plantation on their horses, occasionally stopping along the river to sit on the banks and talk. Afterwards, they would return home for breakfast and then retreat to the front porch where they would sit and chew tobacco. Neither of them held any regard for the slaves as they made it a point to be nasty and make life difficult for them. No spit ever made it to the spittoon, nor did they lift a finger to do anything else.

Their stately home was two high levels over a twelve-foot basement. The upper stories were of beautiful pink brick that had taken several months to plaster. There was no cohesion or conformity in its wings, except in color and massive bulk. Two overpowering sets of four Corinthian columns rose upward to an enlarged entablature of horizontal lines and large dentils. One set of columns was pedimental, and the other was not. Intricately carved capitals made from solid blocks of cypress were themselves six feet tall. The main portions of the house were tied together by the large entablature with its dentils, which were simulated on the rounded turrets. The wings had

Roman arched window openings, while regular framed windows of various widths were used elsewhere. Most of the rooms had narrow balconies, and sometimes on warm gentle nights, Silas and Massa Gray would sit out there in their underwear drinking wine and could be seen locked in fervent kisses. Inside and out there was a profusion of pilasters and columns. Internal frieze work and decorations were abundant. All of the doorknobs and keyhole covers were silver in color, with every aspect of the building and furnishing elaborate beyond compare.

❋❋❋

During the summer of 1820, Silas went to Charleston to meet a cargo ship that had come in from the West Indies. His purpose there was to buy four or five more slaves to work around the house. At the auction, he, along with other planters, realized most of the chattel seemed sickly, but he managed to find four that would fit in nicely with the rest. Over the years, they had amassed several hundred slaves and remained one of the largest plantations in Savannah. Before he could return home, two of the slaves died, and he dumped their bodies on the side of the road. Shortly after he got back to the plantation, the other two died as well. Just as they had done to others, their bodies were burned.

A week later, Silas took sick. Massa Gray, at first, had their house servants bringing him cool water and bowls of ice to bring his fever down. Silas was dripping wet with sweat every minute of the day and could barely muster enough strength to get in and out of his clothes. Then the vomiting started, and it was black in color. His eyes, ears, pores and nose began to run blood almost constantly. At that point, Massa Gray sent for the doctor. When the doctor arrived, he observed Silas's symptoms, placed his stethoscope back in his bag, and asked, "Has he been anywhere near Charleston lately?"

Massa Gray replied, "Well, yes, he went there a couple of weeks ago for an auction."

"I see. Did he bring anything back with him?"

"Why, yes, he did, but two of them died before he could get them back here."

"Where are the others?"

"They died about a week ago."

"I see. What did you do with the bodies?"

There was no way Massa Gray was going to admit what they had done with the bodies. "I had couple of the field hands bury them in the cemetery down by the slave quarters. What is it, doctor?"

The doctor walked over to the ceramic basin and washed his hands feverishly. "In many port cities, there has been an outbreak of yellow fever, and I believe that's what Silas has. It's highly contagious, and, well, I can't do any more for him, Theron."

In all his life, Massa Gray had only experienced one love, and it had been Silas. It was like lightning had ripped through him. "You mean you're going to just let him die?"

"Theron," he said, drying his hands against his trousers, "I am not letting him die. The disease moves fast and seems to have been eating away at him for quite some time. I hate to say it, but it's likely everyone on this plantation is going to succumb to it."

"What?"

Picking up his bag, the doctor, who was only a few years older than Silas, said, "I suggest you do what you can to keep him comfortable because he doesn't have much time." With that, he grabbed his hat and left the house.

⊛⊛⊛

For several hours, Massa Gray sat in a chair next to the bed, watching the man he'd grown to love with all his heart give in to death. Taking whatever risk necessary, he moved to the bed. Facing his best friend, he rested his head on Silas's chest and began sobbing.

"Don't do that," Silas whispered. "Don't let them see you do that."

Wiping the water from his face, Massa Gray whimpered softly, "I don't care what they see anymore. I can't lose you."

As a small cough turned into a brutal sign of his weakness by the excreting of blood, Silas said, "You don't have any control over that." A servant took a wet cloth and cleaned the blood from the corners of his mouth. "My time here is done."

"You damn niggers! This is all your fault! Get out! Get the hell out and don't come back!" Massa Gray yelled.

The servants stood there, looking at one another as if they were confused about the orders. Accustomed to Massa Gray's temper, they remained in place.

"Are you too fucking stupid to understand? Get out!"

"Yessuh," they replied as they backed out the door.

⊛⊛⊛

Finally alone, Massa Gray crawled into the bed with Silas and lifted his frail body to where it rested upon his own. He put his arms around Silas and cradled him like an infant. "I can't do this without you," he cried.

Staring down the hall and out the window, Silas's life flashed before him, and it ended with Massa Gray right by his side. "Then don't." He sighed, falling limp in Massa Gray's arms as his eyes rolled to the back of his head.

❁❁❁

Theron Allen Gray sat that evening and wept louder and harder than any man could, over the loss of the love of his life. He got up from the bed and walked toward the window, noticing the peacefulness that had overcome the plantation. Kissing Silas's forehead, he said his good-bye and went downstairs to the basement where they kept barrels of imported whale oil. He poured gallons of it into buckets, loaded them into a one-horse cart, and, as quietly as he could, rode down to the slave quarters. Surrounded by trees and cotton fields at every turn, there were twenty cabins on the female side, and twenty cabins on the male side. He went to every trough and drained the water and next dumped out pails of any standing water he could find. Then Massa Gray took those buckets of whale oil and poured the liquid over everything he could find—porches, laundry, hay, anything. After all of the buckets were emptied, he struck a match and lit clothes that were hanging on a clothesline attached to adjoining cabins, and turned to walk away.

Upon returning to the house, Massa Gray could hear the screams and cries in the night and listened as one life after another vanished. Consumed in his own anguish, Massa Gray went through the house and snatched down every piece of fabric he could find and took it with him to the basement where he struck another match, igniting everything in sight. He ran for the stairs to make his way back to where he had left Silas and climbed into the bed with him.

"I love you," he said solemnly. "We will rot in hell together."

5

W hen love is lost, nothing else matters—not even life. Many of Hattie's days after Quincy's death were spent in solitude and unhappiness. She spent hours sitting alone in her cabin, eating little food and with no desire to maintain life.

Risella, feeling as though she and Litton were to blame for things being the way they were, kept Josiah in the big house and began raising him with Annie. Litton had no objection to the arrangement but insisted Risella keep the matter out of the ears and mouths of the other families they socialized with. It was strange how Litton wore a different mask in public than the one he wore at home. Hattie, who had experienced firsthand what the "other" Litton was capable of, stayed a comfortable distance from him in spite of the opportunity he had afforded Josiah.

Daily, Josiah went to his mother's cabin to spend time with her and to help with some of the small chores around the cabin. Risella had begun to teach him how to read and write but made him promise not to let a soul know about it. At the age of seven, Josiah was reading complete passages from the Bible and knew how to write his name.

"Mama, let me show what I can do," he said one afternoon, while he had been sitting with Hattie. He pulled out a small Bible and began, "When Jesus…"

Suddenly, his mother slapped him across the mouth with an open palm, sending him tumbling out of his chair and onto the floor. "Don't nevah lets anotha nigger knowed you can read," Hattie scolded. "Not me. Not nobody." As she stood over Josiah, who had tearfully picked up his chair and his Bible, Hattie's hatred for Litton blazed in her eyes.

Sniffling, Josiah replied, "Mama, what did I do? Miss Risella…"

"Boy, does I needs to slap ya agin fa tryin' to sass me?"

"No, ma'am," he said, wiping his nose with the sleeve of his shirt. "I only wanted you to be proud of me."

Hattie pulled Josiah into her arms and squeezed him tight. "I'se proud uh ya, Josiah. I jes don want nuthin' to hap-n te ya. All white folks ain't lak Miss Risella."

Young and only eager to learn, Josiah answered, "Yes, ma'am."

❈❈❈

Much of their time was spent in silence with Hattie moping about the cabin and staring out the window. Rejecting the Fews offer to live in the big house, Hattie had more luxuries than the other servants. Unlike the cabins of the other slaves in the quarters, hers was free of holes, broken boards, and rotten wood. Risella had given her a small cot with sheets and blankets, a potbelly stove, and pieces of furniture for her cabin. Josiah, standing there in a clean shirt, trousers, and gently worn shoes, was the spitting image of his father, which sometimes made it difficult for Hattie to even look at him. Then, at other times, it was that image that made her take him into her arms and never let him go.

"'Bout time you head on back te de house. Itz gittin' dark."

"Yes, ma'am," Josiah said, gathering his belongings. "I will see you tomorrow."

❁❁❁

With the rain falling heavily across the grounds, the smoke stack on Hattie's cabin signaled she was awake and that she was waiting for Josiah. When he did not see it the next day, he knew something was wrong. "Miss, have you seen my mama today?"

Risella usually saw Hattie in the mornings picking sunflowers, and, while their relationship had somewhat deteriorated since Quincy's death, Hattie managed a few words every now and then. It had been three years since they'd last had a lengthy conversation. They were in the peach orchard while Hattie was picking peaches for preserves, and Hattie was handing them to Risella, who was arranging the fruit in a basket as the children played only a few feet away.

"I know you're angry with us, Hattie," Risella said, taking a peach from Hattie as she stood on a wooden box to lift her closer to the branches. "I understand how you could be."

Hattie continued snatching peaches from the branches and never looked toward Risella. "Miss, I loves dat man ya husbin had kilt out dare in dat barn. Won't nevah loves lak dat agin. I'se don thank ya could e'ah feels wut I'se feels. Ya ain't lived long enough to feels de kinda pain I'se got in my hart," she said, tossing away one with too much green on it.

"I could say I'm sorry for what Litton did, but it won't bring

Quincy back. You have to know they were going to kill us, if he hadn't told them where Quincy was."

Still plucking peaches from the branches, Hattie panted. "Mighta not. Killin' ya won't gon givs dem Quincy no fasser. Gardless te whedder er not you wuz dead, dey wuz gon get 'em. Dere wuz mo' ya coulda dun to protek 'em."

Risella knew she was probably right. "Hattie, dear, I wish things could go back to the way they were between you and me. You seem so angry all the time."

Knowing she would never allow things to go back to the way they used to be, Hattie said, "Us gives up our freedum te comes and works for dat man's fader and mudder. I'se not angry, miss, jes hart broke. Dat's all. Massa wuz not right fa wut he did sens his fader say he was gon protek us down here in Joe-gee. I dun forgives 'em fa it, but it hard te forgit it."

Defeated, Risella asked, "Is there not anything I can do?"

Pausing as she pulled another ripened peach from the branch, Hattie said, "Dey's one thang you can do fa me and Quincy."

Getting up from the ground and dusting off the back of her dress, Risella eagerly asked, "What is it, Hattie?"

Looking deep into the orchard, watching Annie and Josiah play like brother and sister, she responded, "Jes do right by my boy."

Hattie didn't expect an answer from Risella because she knew it was something she could not promise. At that point, an apology wasn't necessary, and Hattie hadn't expected one either.

❊❊❊

Risella glanced over at Josiah, who had a puzzled look on his face. He lived for those daily visits with his mother; even though their relationship seemed strained from time to time. Josiah, too young to try to figure out how to compete with his mother's pain, remained constant in his efforts to strengthen his ties to his mother. Raised mostly by the Fews, he didn't know what being a servant was really like until later in life. No matter how Litton felt about it, Risella made sure Josiah would have a life worth something.

"I haven't seen her today, Josiah. Since it's raining outside, maybe she's resting."

For as long as he could remember, Josiah knew his mother picked sunflowers every day, rain or shine. "No, miss, she picks flowers every day. Something is wrong."

Containing her concern so as to not alarm Josiah, Risella, who was washing off some apples, agreed that something was not right. "Josiah, dear, I'm sure everything is fine. I will go down there with you to show you that she's fine."

One thing Risella knew about Hattie was that she never broke her routine with those flowers.

Many, many times before, Risella had walked down to Hattie's cabin, and it had taken only a few minutes. This time, however, it seemed more like a long, long journey. Holding Josiah's hand, Risella squeezed it every few seconds for comfort as the boy stumbled across rocks and holes that he had passed with ease all the other times.

Just steps away from the cabin, Josiah stopped dead in his tracks and yanked twice on Risella's hand. "Can you go in there and see first?"

There was still no smoke coming from the chimney. Kneeling down to where she was eye-to-eye with Josiah, Risella said assuredly, "Yes, I can do that."

She released her hand from his and proceeded to the steps of the cabin. Once inside, she found Hattie lying on the cot with a bunch of freshly picked sunflowers clutched in her hands; finally at peace.

❁❁❁

By the time he was ten years old, Josiah knew more words and read better than most White men in Augusta. Risella had taught both him and Annie about proper manners and spent a great deal of time giving them history, math, and writing lessons. A fast and eager learner, Josiah wanted very much to spread his knowledge to the other slaves on the plantation but quickly remembered what his mother had told him. Therefore, he stayed as close to the big house as he possibly could. While still trying to provide some type of positive influence for Josiah, Litton kept his distance from the situation to prevent the ridicule and harassment of his family. If anyone found out they were harboring a nigger who could read and write, it would ruin their business relationships and drive off their friends. It was one thing to raise an orphan, but it was another to raise a nigger who might end up being better than you.

Josiah's relationship with Annie was one of pure innocence—at first. Hattie had nursed Annie, and when necessary and no one else was around, Risella had nursed Josiah. That was one of many secrets they'd kept between themselves. Isolated from the cruelty of the outside, Annie and Josiah created their own world where there was no such thing as one person being better than the other. Every piece of cake or pie Annie had she shared with him, and he did the same. One afternoon when Litton had come in from a business trip to Texas where they had begun to export cotton from his crops, he was asked by Annie to come and observe a game that she and Josiah had been playing. Taking a seat in the parlor, he listened as the children giggled and ran about the house, getting ready for the activity. The next time he saw Annie, she was wearing a white dress, and Josiah entered the room behind her in a pair of nice trousers, braces, and a shirt.

"Look, Papa, Josiah and I are getting married." She laughed.

Not at all amused by the display, Litton grabbed Annie by the arm and demanded, "Where's your mother, young lady?"

"Owww, Papa, you're hurting me," Annie whined. "She's down in the orchard picking peaches for dessert."

Litton stormed out the house and headed straight for the orchard, where he found Risella going through a bushel of peaches, tossing out the bruised ones. She looked up and saw her husband approaching her with the steam of a raging bull behind him.

"What on earth's wrong, Litton? You look like…"

"He's got to go out to the quarters with the others."

"What are you talking about?" Risella asked as she tried to wipe a bead of sweat from Litton's forehead, but he pushed her hand away.

"It's time for Josiah to mix in with his own kind," he said.

"What has happened?" she asked frantically. "I left them alone in the house while I came out here. For God's sake, they're children and couldn't have gotten into much that quickly."

"They're in there playing like they're about to be married. What kind of nonsense is that? Do you know what kind of trouble we could get in around here, if someone else had come in the house with me?"

"My word, Litton. They are only children. Fortunately for

them, they don't see this old, ugly world as you and I do. Just let them be."

"I can't do that, Risella. It's too risky. He will be going outside with the others just as soon as I can get back up to the house. We can put him in his folks' old cabin. That way he'll be close enough for you to look after him," he said firmly. The rest of the slaves were a quarter of a mile away.

Thinking back to the day she and Hattie had stood almost in the very same spot, Risella refuted, "I can't let that happen, Litton. I promised his mother I'd look after him, and, besides, he's only a child."

"I don't care what you promised her. He's old enough to look after himself. You can check on him whenever you want."

"No!" she cried. "You may not have murdered his father, but you got his blood on your hands just the same. I am not going to let you send him out into the world because you say so."

"The way I see it is you have a choice. Either peacefully take him and his belongings out to the cabin, or he goes forcefully and you go with him." In all their years together, Litton had never taken that tone with his wife.

"I can't believe you would do and say such things to me; after all I've been to you. I've watched you cavorting with these, these *monsters* you call men, and you didn't used to be this way. After you've swapped a few stories about your 'darkies' and your 'niggers' like it's some kind of sport, you come back here and call us all one, happy family. Around here you tell them they are not your slaves, but out there in the real world, you sell them out just like you sell your cotton," she protested as her voice trembled. "As I am not a hypocrite such as you, I will sleep in the cabin with Josiah so he won't think he's all alone in this cruel, White man's world." Risella picked up the basket and headed back to the house, leaving Litton behind.

❖❖❖

After walking for some time to gather his thoughts, Litton returned home to find Risella's trunk packed and waiting by the door. He hadn't counted on Risella taking him seriously about her moving into the cabin with Josiah. He never once figured she would give up the lavish lifestyle to which she'd grown accustomed, nor did he think that Risella would take pleasure in sleeping away from him. Looking around the lower level of the house, Litton saw nothing out of the ordinary. The servants were busy in the kitchen preparing for supper, and Annie and Josiah were out in the backyard playing as they normally did that time of day. He went upstairs to see if Risella was still around because he desperately needed to talk with his wife. She wasn't in their bedroom nor was she in any of the other bedrooms. As he prepared to head downstairs, he heard footsteps upstairs in the nursery. He ran through the kitchen past the boiling pots and pans and went out the back door to the servant's steps. Taking two steps at a time, Litton made it to the landing and found Risella putting Josiah's things into a small case.

"Risella, please wait," he pleaded softly.

Never looking up at her husband, Risella said, shaking her head, "Litton, we don't have anything to talk about."

Watching Risella neatly place Josiah's shirts and books into the case, Litton continued, "I love you, and I was wrong for what I said out there."

Still moving about the room, Risella asked, "Wrong about which part? The part about Josiah needing to be with his own kind, or the part about me having to go out to the cabin to stay with him?"

Clearing his throat, Litton, who was never one to admit his errors, said, "You know I don't desire my wife to sleep out in the slave quarters. That's dehumanizing."

Risella finally paused in astonishment. "What?"

"Having you out there is not right. That environment is not meant for...well, you know."

"Whites?"

"Well, yes. They," he said as he pointed toward Josiah as he played in the backyard, "are used to it and can survive out there. They're like monkeys in a jungle." He chuckled.

"Litton Few! What ever is wrong with you?" she demanded, slamming the case shut.

"Look, this foolishness must stop. You will not be moving your things from this house. Josiah can stay only during the day, but he must return to his cabin at night. Oh, and he and Annie need to stop spending so much time together. It doesn't look good."

"I can't believe you have the nerve to place limits on this family. Annie will play with whomever she wants, and, before I subject that innocent little boy to your rules, I will take my things and my daughter to the cabin and stay as long as I please."

Furious with his wife's defiance, Litton surprisingly agreed, "Fine, go ahead then, but Annie will stay here. No daughter of mine will ever live like that."

"Fine then, but you can't protect her from the world forever."

❖❖❖

Four years passed, and Risella stayed firm in her promise to Hattie and continued to look after Josiah. During the day, she increased his studies by teaching him Spanish and by allowing him to read the local newspaper from time to time. It was there where he learned about the world and used that knowledge to keep him focused on the injustice of slaves everywhere. His strength, however, seemed to be of a political nature, and Risella noticed this right away. With what little she knew about politics, she provided him with the best answers she could. One afternoon while flipping through a history book, Josiah stumbled upon a poster that had been carefully folded and placed in the back of the book. Opening the discolored paper, he discovered a description of his mother and father and immediately took it to Risella who was out in the garden picking vegetables for dinner. "They were runaways?" he asked softly as he calmly lowered the paper to where she was knelt on the ground.

Cleaning her hands against her dress, Risella took the paper and glanced over it, clearly dismissing the images and words printed on it. "Josiah, I think it's time you and I have a talk." She sighed as she lifted her hand for him to help her up from the ground. "Come take a walk with me." Risella chose to walk through the orchard because it was near autumn and no one would be out there. They walked to the farthest side where no one could see or hear them. "You're old enough now to know the truth about your parents, and I brought you out here for your own protection."

"Yes, ma'am."

The sun was at its highest of the day, and the two sat underneath a tree to shield themselves from it. Risella had grown to love Josiah as if he was her own son and had done everything in her power to protect him from the ways of the White man, but she knew she couldn't do that forever. "Sometimes I feel responsible for your father's death. It was I who knew they were runaways and didn't do anything to protect them. I didn't tell my husband when I should have."

Hattie had told Josiah about his father but never placed any blame on the Fews, as a whole, for his death, even though she did hold it against Litton. It was always her contention that Silas and Massa Gray might have killed Quincy, but Litton gave them the noose.

"God has His own way of doing things, Miss Risella, and it's not for us to question. If my father had still been here, then I wouldn't have had the years I've had with you. I forgave Master Litton a long time ago."

Risella, who had finally begun to show signs of age with two patches of graying hair on both sides of her temple, smiled at Josiah, taking his hand in hers. "I promised your mother I would take care of you."

"And you've been doing that most graciously."

Much of Josiah's day was spent in or around the cabin. Although he had been to the cotton fields on the other side of the plantation a few times, Risella insisted he stay where she could keep up with him. Many of the slaves did not like Josiah because of the special treatment he got from the Fews and would do anything to jeopardize his place amongst the others. Whenever he was around the other servants, he made it a point to not say much or nothing at all. The extent of his words to them was "yes ma'am," "no ma'am," "yessuh," and "no suh."

"Well, you still have a lifetime in front of you, and I'm going to make sure it's spent for the good of making you into a better man."

Wincing at the brightness of the sun's rays, Josiah asked, "Miss Risella?"

"Yes, dear?"

"Are all Negroes slaves?"

"No, they are not. Up North, they are free." She winked.

"I guess then, I..."

Risella quickly put her fingers to Josiah's mouth. "I know, Josiah. I know."

❁❁❁

Litton had softened a bit and allowed Annie to visit her mother when she was not doing her studies. Annie's relationship with her mother was rather strong; despite the fact that she wasn't in the big house with her. They walked together through the orchard and talked about everything from boys to school to new friends.

"How's Josiah?" Annie asked one evening, as she and Risella walked back toward the house. "I don't' get to see him much when Papa's around."

"He's getting along just fine."

Checking to the side and back of her for her father, Annie said, "I sure miss him. We used to have such fun together."

"I'm certain he misses you, too. One day I might arrange for you two to have tea down by the orchard; when your father is not in town."

"I would like that very much."

"Consider it done then."

❁❁❁

Those secret meetings happened as frequently as once a week when Litton was away on business, and it was the only time Josiah had a genuine smile on his face. The two talked about things as complicated as their studies but as simple as the exportation of cotton and its continued expansion into other states. Neither of them cared much for it because, without the hard work of the Fews' "servants," their crop wouldn't even exist.

"I wish we could both run away to the North, where Negroes are free," Annie blurted out one afternoon. "I hate living here sometimes."

"I know how you feel, Miss Annie, but I'd never run away and risk getting caught. They kill folks like me. God has a plan for me, and I'm going to wait on Him."

Josiah's comments were nothing but admirable to Annie. "I can respect that. You know, we've been doing this for a few months now, and I think Papa is getting suspicious." Even when Litton was home, Annie had not been able to resist spending time with Josiah. "He's started asking me where I've been and who I was with. I don't want you to get into trouble because of me," she said.

"I understand, but I'm willing to take that chance, Miss Annie. This time we spend together is more than words could ever mean to me. If I get caught, then I will proudly sacrifice my freedom, for it would have been worth everything to me." Josiah stretched out on his back across the grass and crossed his ankles in comfort.

Blushing at Josiah's words, Annie, now approaching the age of sixteen, said, "Those are beautiful words, Josiah. I never knew you could express yourself so eloquently." And then without warning, Annie took a deep breath, closed her eyes, and lowered her head and pressed her lips against Josiah's. The kiss lasted for many seconds as Annie tried to fight the passion rising in her but couldn't.

Pulling Josiah to her, she wrapped her arms around his waist as he took her face into his hands. Annie's gentle moans turned into short pants while her hands slid down around Josiah's backside, and his hands found their way beneath her dress. He grabbed her, forcing his hands between her legs to take hold of the one thing that could mean an instant end to his life.

"Miss Annie," Josiah called out softly, with his lips now against her cheeks. "We must stop. Life would never be the same for either of us if someone sees what's going on, and I don't want that for you or for me."

"But, Josiah, I want to. No one even knows we're out here."

Josiah, a young man of great dignity and respect, said as he rubbed his cheek against hers, "I can't, Miss Annie. Please don't be angry with me for caring about you."

Disappointed, Annie responded, "I thank you for that."

"I think we should not see each other any more for a while," he said hesitantly. "With how I feel about you, I can't say that I will always be able to exhibit such restraint."

"I understand."

From that moment on, it was hard to determine where their friendship was headed. Annie would see him from afar and wave to him, but often got nothing in return. She would send for him, but when he got to her, he had nothing to offer by way of conversation.

While Annie had developed a new circle of friends, Litton did not allow Josiah at the house when they had visitors, and when he did visit, he did not want the two alone together at any time. Risella came to the house when Litton had planned fancy dinner parties and played her part as missus the very best she could. But, the minute the last guest left the house, Risella went back out to the cabin. On Sundays after church, Risella ate dinner with the family and eventually talked Litton into letting Josiah eat with them. But Litton, although he agreed to Josiah's presence, refused to acknowledge him when he was at the table. Josiah had grown tired of trying to be respectful toward Litton, and, after a while, he took his Sunday dinner out in the cabin.

6

Annie Few Smith, known for her quiet disposition and sometimes timid composure, stepped onto the back porch and directly into the scorching Georgia heat. Usually white as talcum powder during the winter months, her cheeks were red like strawberries from her daily, late summer walks to the edge of the plantation where the cotton fields simply dropped off into the horizon. Looking over the pastures and fields as her husband's slaves toiled in the blistering sun, the blue-eyed Annie searched for her best friend, Lisbeth Olson Brown, who was due any minute for their afternoon tea. Between them, they had shared everything, but their social differences had separated them over the years, and Annie, while she reflected on what had gotten her to this point, had decided it was time for them to part ways. With the secret she held within, she knew the end of their friendship was inevitable.

❖❖❖

Throughout their formative years, Annie and Lisbeth had done what all young girls do at some point—dreamed of their wedding days. Together, they had planned to marry the two richest men in Augusta. Each afternoon they spent their moments of innocence constantly trying to outdo one another with fancy wedding decorations. Lisbeth, devoted to Southern traditions and customs, was determined to have a house full of servants and own land farther than the eye could see. She was much like her mother, a simple woman named Miss Lucy who was overtly jealous of the wives in her husband's circle of friends. She and her husband, Reverend Jake, owned only six slaves while their other friends owned fifty or more. Reverend was a firm believer in it only taking a few good niggers to make his plantation work, and too many of them would eat into any profits he'd make from his crops.

He let Miss Lucy work the ones in the house like dogs, and he was just as bad because he worked the ones in the fields like there was no tomorrow for them. The missus was all about how things looked on the outside and not about what they really were on the inside. True enough, the Olsons did not have much money, although they lived comfortably, but you couldn't tell it by the way Miss Lucy made her husband spend it. One time Mr. Odell Winsome, one of Reverend Jake's friends from church, bought his wife a silk bedspread that they said came from France. After Miss Lucy made such a fuss about it, Jake managed to buy that same bedspread for his wife. The wicked woman that she was, when she got it, she ripped it from its package and handed it to Easter, her house slave, and told her to put it on the bed. Over in the night, after tossing and turning all over Jake, she called out to Easter, who she kept on the floor near her during the night in case she wanted a glass of water or cup of hot cider, and told her to take the spread from the bed and throw it away because it made her itch. Not once did she utter a "thank you" to her husband. The expensive bedspread ended up on the floor with Easter.

Reverend Jake had a good ole heart, but his love for his wife managed to put a hole in it. In reality, Miss Lucy had everything a White man's wife could want—slaves, a fine house, and a little bit of status. In theory, though, she really had nothing. Her husband's associates—self-proclaimed politicians and slave enthusiasts who were drawn to the Olsons because, at the time, they were one of only a few Georgians that had some early success in cotton—were cordial with his wife but refrained from holding much conversation with her. Miss Lucy's spirit was often cold and counterfeit. She was feared by each of her slaves—particularly her house servants—because she had a temper that could attack like a rattlesnake. One minute she would praise the slaves for being good niggers and in the next, she would hit them with her stick yelling, "You ain't never supposed to look your missus in the eye!"

Her actions and attitudes were the same with Lisbeth. Once the poor child was locked outside stark naked while Reverend Jake was away because she would not put on the dress her mother wanted her to wear. After Miss Lucy drifted off for her afternoon nap, Easter crept outside and made good use of that silk bedspread by wrapping Lisbeth up in it and walking her to Annie's for some tea and fresh air. Upon her arrival, Annie gave Lisbeth a dress and a cup of hot tea. Trembling from fear and embarrassment, Lisbeth sipped the tea, staring hopelessly at the ground. That was the only time they ever had teatime in silence. As Lisbeth prepared to return home, Annie folded up the bedspread, but Lisbeth immediately refused it, saying, "I don't want any parts of that ol' dusty thing. Throw it away, if you want.

That nigger, Easter, sleeps with it, and I never want to see it
again."

Annie loved family heirlooms and valued every piece of her
English heritage by salvaging whatever memories of London
she could get her hands on. "Do you not know what this is?"

"Yes, I do. It's a dirty ol' rag the niggers sleep on, and I don't
need it."

"It's French silk, Lisbeth. The finest money can buy, actually.
My grandparents had one of these, and…"

"Annie, my gosh, just take the damn thing!" Lisbeth yelled.
"The only thing it's good for, at this point, is a cover beneath
the horses to catch their business." She cackled as she got her
belongings together. "I must get on home now, before Mama
wakes up."

❖❖❖

It was no secret that Reverend Jake Olson had a lady friend.
Even Miss Lucy knew about Miss Frances who lived down by
the creek that ran next to town. Everybody knew that when
Lucy was on a tear, they could find Reverend Jake at Miss
Frances's. Before too long, Reverend Jake tired of Miss Lucy
and had her servants pack her belongings. Gently, he told her,
"You are no longer welcome here, Lucy. There's a carriage waiting for you at the end of the orchard but Lisbeth stays here with
me." As simple as that, Miss Lucy was out and moved away somewhere up North.

Lisbeth's years with her father were not the best for her.
Because she was a constant reminder of the former Mrs. Olson,
Miss Frances rarely spoke to her, leaving the child to be raised

by the slaves that worked in and around the house. Despite their loyalty to her, Lisbeth mistreated the servants just as most of the other White folks did. Even though she and Annie shared some things in common, their morals regarding slavery were the one divisive issue between them. Annie, educated by private tutors from London, adopted the abolitionists' sympathetic views toward slavery. Her family never mistreated their servants. They fed them well and made sure they had proper clothing. As a result, none of their help ever tried to escape. The servants were not there for show or status. Their purpose was to help Litton prepare his land for his cotton crops. Miss Lisbeth was a jealous woman who couldn't stand seeing Annie and her family having more than she. She was mean to the servants, often forgetting she was not in charge at Fews Grove. Litton once advised her that she had better fix her tongue or she would no longer be welcome at his house. One day ,while she and Annie were playing out in the meadow, Miss Lisbeth threw her hands on top of her hips and sassed,

"I got one...

"You got two...

"When I grow up I'm gonna have more niggers than you."

"Lisbeth Olson, why on earth would you say something so cruel?" Annie inquired, frowning.

"Because it's true. One day I *am* going to have more slaves than you. I'm going to have more money than you, too."

"Silly, girl." Annie giggled. "Is that all you think about, Lisbeth? Having more than me? I mean, we are friends and have been for a long time. I don't sit around and measure what you don't have to what I do have. That's not how it should be. We have servants...not slaves. The only reason my father won't set them free is because keeping them here and happy is the only way to protect them from the likes of people like you."

"You just a ol' nigger lover; that's all. You let them say and do whatever they want to around you. Your mama even works out there with them."

Taking Miss Lisbeth by the hand, Annie replied softly, "They are people just like we are, my friend. They breathe like we do, they hurt like we do, and they love like we do, too. I wish..."

Astonished by Annie's sincere words, Miss Lisbeth scowled, "How dare you let words like that come from your mouth? Any White person besides me ever hears you say such awful things, they would..."

"Would what, Lisbeth? Go on, say it!" she said, yanking her hand from Miss Lisbeth's.

"They'd wash your mouth out with soap and make you sleep with them, out there in their quarters." She laughed. "Bet you change your mind then."

Annie had no desire to debate the issue any further with Miss Lisbeth. Her friend was who she was. There was no changing her.

❁❁❁

Winning the heart of Lieutenant Royce Smith—a young, Southern gentleman whose family's earnings first came from the rice industry, Lisbeth was relegated to watching Annie snag the kind of man they had always talked about. A graduate of West Point, Royce was a fast-talking, slightly stout man. When he first met Annie at church, he could not keep away from her, constantly trying to impress her with flowers and chocolates, but Annie was always the lady and never accepted his advances.

During church service when the men would discuss how the slaves were supposed to obey their masters because that was what the Bible instructed, Royce would be the first one to speak up in agreement. Annie would turn her head in disgust. After a while, Royce quieted a bit, but only long enough for Annie to invite him over for tea. Lisbeth was incensed with jealousy. Sometimes she would show up and disrupt their conversation by plopping herself right in between them. Ever the busybody, she never minded her business and always made it a point to tell Annie how handsome and rich Royce was. "You better watch how you're treating him, Annie. There are plenty of women out here who could treat him right," she would always say.

❁❁❁

Royce and Annie had a fancy wedding, just like the one she had planned when she was a young girl. No matter how nice he treated his new wife, she didn't like the fact that he had slaves, and Annie knew that, like the others, he could be cruel when he wanted to be. As a wedding gift, he divided his chattel evenly with Annie, but she refused to take ownership of them and threatened to set them free since they were now *her* property. She even insisted that the proper papers be filed so there would not be any trouble later on. Then, just as quickly as he had given them to her, he had taken them back. Any of them that she had grown extremely fond of, Royce sold for little or nothing to his friends who lived as far away as Montgomery, Alabama. Annie, though heartbroken with her husband's cruelty, manifested her love in the remaining ones; particularly—Ina and Susie.

Lisbeth compromised her childhood dream of wealth and

prosperity for what she thought to be true love and eventually married a tall, thin, balding man. They had met at a garden party given by Annie and Royce to celebrate Royce's new political affiliation with the Whig party. Will Brown, a loner from Savannah, did not have much money. Lisbeth was a woman of medium build with reddish blonde hair and stood just above her husband's six-foot frame. Ridden with an often unpleasant childhood, she looked well beyond her years of only twenty-four.

Will Brown was a tenant farmer who grew cotton on the Smith's land. Instead of paying Royce Smith in cash, the Browns requested use of a few slaves to tend to the crops and to help Lisbeth around the house. Royce gave them Ina and Susie. Despite Annie's efforts to protect her, Ina, at the age of sixteen, had already borne three children for Royce. Her job was to cook, clean the house and tend to Lisbeth. Ina was thankful to be leaving the Smith plantation because it had become a nightly ritual for the overseer to drag her out of her cabin to a waiting one-horse cart that raced through the darkness to a fireside campsite where Royce was waiting for her.

Will Brown, however, did not care for sleeping with the niggers. His primary interest was his cotton. Whenever Lisbeth was not feeling up to being with him in a natural way, she sent him down to the slave quarters to find comfort in Ina. His wife felt that doing this would help them have some darkies of their own. For Lisbeth, everything was about status and finally being able to have a smidgen of the wealth afforded Annie. Some say she was jealous of Mrs. Smith because she had it all—a successful husband, status, beauty and a plantation full of servants devoted to her every need. Lisbeth and Will took what they could get.

None of that mattered much to Will, but it made his wife furious that she could not have the life she always wanted.

❂❂❂

Ina, born somewhere in Louisiana close to the Mississippi line, was torn from her mother's arms by speculators when she was a baby. Back then, they would come in the night and steal babies; right from their mother's breast if they had to. At that time, Ina's mother tried to run after the one that had got hold of Ina, and another man on a horse came up from behind and trampled her. None of them ever looked back. Royce's father, Merriweather, bought the child from them for her to play with Royce's niece, Jessica, who was around twenty years younger than he was at the time. Jessica and Ina played together throughout Jessica's childhood, but when Ina got to be twelve years old, Merriweather gave her to Royce as a wedding gift. "Ain't nothing like a nigger wench that ain't been spoiled," he said, right in front of Annie.

Later that night, before they consummated their marriage, Annie, dressed in a lace gown that showed off all the gifts she had for her new husband, asked, "Royce, dear, you don't intend to have your way with that little girl, do you?"

Stunned, Royce paused as he slipped out of his pants. "No, Annie. My father is a frisky old man and will probably still be thinking dirty when we put him six feet under. He did not mean anything by that. I am not anything like him. Besides, you are right. She is just a girl. What kind of man do you think I am?" he asked as he slid into bed.

Annie knew what kind of man he was. She had married a

slave owner—a man who, on Sundays while in the Lord's house, bragged about his sexual prowess with the female servants on the plantation and about the whippings he would give if anyone disobeyed. There were four mulatto children on the plantation. Each of them bore a striking resemblance to Royce.

Putting her long, silky black hair beneath her nightcap, she replied, "You should not ask me about the man that I think you are. It is the man I know you are that worries me." Annie rested her slender body against the back of the bed.

Royce, nude beneath the sheets, tried to pull Annie to him, but she sat there like a stubborn mule. He tried to lift her arms so he could take her out of her gown, but she kept her arms tight to her side.

"Annie, are we going to do this on our wedding night? I want you, honey. I really do." He gave her a quick, little kiss on the cheek and then pressed a longer one on her forehead. "I've been waiting a long time for you."

Realizing he was right about it being their wedding night, Annie stopped resisting and began returning Royce's gestures. She allowed him to mount her across her thighs, resting his manhood in the split in between. His passionate, wet kisses made their way around her neck and down to her breasts, and he circled the peaks with his tongue and like a child to its mammy, he embraced them with his mouth. Annie wrapped her arms around his waist, sliding into the sheets while he simultaneously lifted her nightdress. Their passionate moans welcomed one another as they exchanged pelvic thrusts and heat. Royce gently slid himself between Annie's thighs, banishing all thoughts that he was a slave owner, and made her remember only the fact that he was her husband.

7

In their first year of marriage, Royce tried really hard to make Annie give in to having slaves working for her around the plantation, but no matter what he said, she objected. "You will do as I say around here, Annie. This ain't your folks' place, where your mother ran things," he told her.

The very next morning Annie set out to talk with her mother, who still lived in the cabin with Josiah. "Mama, I can't allow myself to have a slave working for me. It goes against everything you taught me. At the same time, I can't continue to disobey my husband."

Just then, Josiah walked in from taking his daily walk down to the river. His eyes lit up when he saw Annie sitting in his favorite chair. "Good morning, Miss Annie. It's so good to see you."

Annie had not seen Josiah since she'd moved to Royce's plantation, and because of the feelings she once had for him, she kept her distance. "Good morning to you, too, Josiah. It's been a many moons since I last saw you," she said.

Josiah had grown as tall as his father, but his muscular frame was thin like his mother's. He looked nothing like the other Negroes who worked around the plantation. His skin was smooth and shiny like molasses, and his clothes were clean and freshly ironed. The most work he ever did was to help Risella chop wood for the stove and take care of the horses used for her carriage. Despite Annie's marriage to Royce, Josiah felt as if Annie's soul belonged to him.

"Yes, I know. We miss seeing you around the place," he said. "They been treating you right?"

Bewildered at Josiah's attention to her because she and Josiah had not spoken in several months, Annie answered, "That's what I came over here to talk with Mama about. Royce, that silly man, insists I have a few servants about the house. I don't need them. I can cook my own food and sew my own clothes. I don't have any children, so I don't need a mammy. The servants who are there now are for his benefit. Not mine." Just like her mother, Annie was as stubborn as a mule.

Josiah pulled up a chair and sat between Annie and Risella. "Miss Annie, don't you need a coachman?"

"A coachman?" she asked.

"Why, yes ma'am, a coachman. I can do that for you." He gleamed.

As much as Annie wanted to have Josiah close to her, she could not risk Royce discovering that the two had a history. "I don't know about that, Josiah," she said, glancing at her mother.

"I think that would be a lovely idea," Risella agreed. "It would give him a chance to do some other things. All Royce is concerned about is having a bunch of Negroes waiting on you so he can impress those poop-for-brains friends of his. I be damned if that's not what you'd be giving him."

"Mama," Annie said sympathetically, "I have never considered Josiah a slave. He never has been, and I think it would be just God-awful to put him in that position. You know how Royce can be."

Reared back in his chair, Josiah gently interjected, "I'd do it for you, Miss Annie."

Annie was afraid of that. Although she and Josiah had been raised together like brother and sister, Annie could not help but go back to the day the two of them had kissed in the orchard. At no other time had she felt such passion and lust for any man. She had never told anyone about that day, and she knew Josiah had done the same.

"Josiah, I simply cannot let you do that for me. I mean, you…"

Risella recognized what was between Josiah and Annie because she, too, had once been in love. Annie's cheeks had turned cherry red, and Josiah's smile never left his face.

"Look, Josiah, if you're sure you want to do this for Annie, then we will have to work on what's proper. Royce is unlike any White man you've ever met. He's mean and nasty when he wants to be, and the last thing you want is him against you."

Josiah answered eagerly, "Yes, ma'am." His heart filled with warmth, for he knew he'd finally be able to spend more time with Annie.

"A word of caution to the both of you," Risella warned.

"Yes?" they questioned simultaneously.

"Don't ever let anybody see the two of you looking at each other like I just saw you look at one another. That man will kill the both of you."

❁❁❁

All through the early summer months of 1835, Royce began to spend a lot of time away from the house, and Annie found herself alone more times than she had wished. She tried to reach out to Lisbeth, but their socio-economic differences made the effort useless. While Lisbeth focused mainly on where and who she wanted to be in life, Annie yearned for someone to simply give attention to the beauty of life, love and friendship. Life for Annie had been governed by her father. He chose how she lived, where she lived, and who she loved. Litton, in spite of the fact Risella detested Royce, encouraged the relationship by boasting of his riches in land and cotton. During the time he courted Annie, Royce raved about the number of slaves he had and how it was because of them he had become so successful in cotton. Litton made sure that his and Annie's surroundings guaranteed she would land the most suitable husband. After the marriage, Litton was most definitely the proud father and knew he had helped Annie to make the right choice. Royce was indeed a businessman, but he also had a firm hand about his house and his plantation. The last thing Litton ever wanted was for his daughter's marriage to end up like his.

Annie was nervous when Josiah met Royce because she did not want Royce to realize their connection. Busy with his own affiliations and such, Royce did not offer any objections. As a matter of fact, he took Josiah out to the stables and told him to pick the two finest horses for Annie's carriage. Royce also got one of his own trusty niggers, John Otis—a blacksmith, to work alongside him. There was to always be two of them on the carriage—the driver and the footman. He had no qualms with who did what, as long as Annie's safety came first. If the horses needed feeding, Josiah did it. If the horses needed shoes, Josiah did it. If anything was wrong with the carriage, then it was up to Josiah to make it right.

Royce finally told him, "Boy, if you have to get out and lay across the road so Miss Annie doesn't have to feel a bump, then you better get your ass out and do it."

Oftentimes while he was away, Royce commanded Josiah to go inside the house and help Annie if and when she needed it. Josiah did not offer much conversation with Royce—for obvious reasons—and Royce was actually delighted at the fact that he finally had a nigger who did not offer any lip. Because of Josiah's loyalty to Annie, Royce's trust level far exceeded what he had for the other slaves, and, for John Otis—who had always done what he had been told to do—that created a problem.

❖❖❖

Annie loved Royce, but not the way a woman was supposed to love her husband; and there were several reasons she could not do so. Of course, there were the simple things—he had deplorable table manners; he carried an odor; he snored; and he did not try to hold meaningful conversations with her. The main reason, however, was his opinion of slavery and how he treated the slaves on his plantation. He whipped them, made them live in horrible conditions, and rarely, if ever, fed them, which is why Annie insisted that Josiah maintain his residence with Risella.

One afternoon in late July, Annie was sitting in a swing out in the yard, trying to read a book. She would read a page or two and then throw the book down in frustration. Picking it back up, she would try again to read a little more, but this time she read aloud. Within a few seconds, the book ended up back on the ground. Annie threw the palms of her hands to her face and wept. Her life was empty, and she had no way of filling it.

"Miss Annie?"

Visibly shaken, Annie flattened her hand above her eyes to block the sun so she could see the face of the man's voice that was unmistakable to her. "Josiah, I didn't hear you come up."

"I didn't mean to startle you. I was coming up to see if you wanted to go into town, or something, since you seem to be having a little trouble," he offered.

"I'm sorry. I didn't think anyone was paying any attention to little ol' me out here," Annie said as she tried to fan a breeze to give her a break from the heat.

Josiah leaned over to pick up her book and handed it back to her. Looking around to see if anyone could see them, he asked, "You want to take that ride, Miss Annie? I can go and fetch John Otis, and we can ride a while. It might cool you off a spell."

"Well, I guess I can, but we don't have to go far, so there's no need to take John Otis with us. Understand?" she persuaded.

"Yes, I understand." Josiah extended his hand to help Annie from the swing and led her to the waiting coach.

❈❈❈

As the carriage swayed from side to side down the clay road, Annie, holding on to her straw garden hat, stuck her head out the window to take in the smell of the fresh honeysuckle and jasmine growing along their way. "Have you ever smelled fresh honeysuckle and jasmine, Josiah?"

"No, Miss Annie, I have not. I imagine it smells divine."

Beaming from ear to ear, Annie replied, "It does." In the distance, Annie saw a meadow where the honeysuckle and jasmine were growing wild. "Josiah, pull over there...right over there by that tree. I want to show you something."

"Yes, ma'am."

"Please don't start that. Royce is nowhere around, so you don't have to be so formal. It's just me."

"Yes...I mean, okay."

❋❋❋

The meadow was actually part of Fews Grove that had never been cultivated. Ambrose insisted the land remain untouched in the event any other Few descendants wanted to build a home there. The edge of the meadow bumped into the banks of the Savannah River; although it was several miles away.

"You know this is my family's land," Annie said as Josiah opened the door and helped her from the coach.

Closing the door, Josiah followed Annie as she began walking through the tall grass. "Really?"

"Yes; it's a little known secret."

"It's beautiful."

Taking in the beauty of nature as far as the eye could see, Annie rushed over to a patch of honeysuckle and jasmine and reached for a handful of them. "Papa can be such an ass sometimes; forever bragging about what we have. While Royce and I were courting, he told him that I would inherit it when he died. You know Royce's eyes got as big as the moon when he heard that." She inhaled as she took a whiff of the flowers and passed them to Josiah. "Don't these smell nice?"

She always jumped from one subject to another and had done so since she was little girl. Josiah was used to it.

Following behind Annie like a little puppy, Josiah approved with the flowers in his hand. "Yes, they do."

He was uneasy about being alone with Annie and gently rested the flowers against the stump of the tree. There was still no one else in sight.

Wearing a simple cotton skirt and matching top with a camisole underneath, Annie pulled Lisbeth's silk blanket from the carriage and spread it over the ground. Then she plopped down on the ground and pulled her body up against the tree, next to the flowers Josiah had placed there.

"Have a seat, Josiah. No one is going to see us out here. Royce is long gone away from here, and nobody else knows about this place. You'll be fine; I promise."

Josiah peeped around the carriage and looked out beyond the greenery to make sure he could see absolutely no one. Just as he was about to sit down, Annie removed her hat and asked him to place it in the carriage. Afterwards, he walked over to where she was sitting and claimed a space a few feet from her. There was a mild breeze coming through the trees, but it did not make much difference with the extreme heat. Butterflies fluttered around them, wild and carefree.

"Those are beautiful creatures—those butterflies," he said as he raised his finger to allow one to land on it.

"Why do you say that?"

Holding his hand steady, he said, "They are the only living creatures that can look at me and not care what I look like. They don't see my color and run from me; nor do they treat me like I'm nothing."

A sadness came from him that Annie had never seen. "Josiah, it has never mattered to me how you look, and I don't run from you. If anything, I run to you because you have always seemed to understand me."

Blushing, Josiah smiled. "That's mighty nice of you, Miss Annie. The only other person that feels like that is Miss Risella. She's always telling me that she's going to make sure I have a better life than what I got."

"If I know my mother, she means it. She's always loved you and has no reason to stop."

"I know, but I get so frustrated with the way things are around here. Your father, since he took sick, doesn't have much to do with me, and Miss Risella is always tending to him so we don't have a lot of time together like we used to."

Giggling, Annie twinkled. "Well, that simply means you have more time to spend with me. You remember that day out in the orchard?"

Josiah remembered that day all too well. "Why, yes I do. It was the day I fell in love with you."

Suddenly, the giggling stopped, and a more serious Annie appeared. "What?"

Prayerfully closing his eyes, with hopes of Annie being able to understand where he was coming from, Josiah professed, "I love you, Miss Annie. That's why I couldn't be around you. When I stopped seeing you, it almost killed me."

Annie knew if anybody heard Josiah speak those things, he would be a dead man, but she also knew they would have to kill her as well. "It's funny you should say such a thing because I love you, too."

Grasping his knees and pulling them into his chest, Josiah began to nervously rock back and forth. He had not expected Annie's words. Clearing his throat, he suggested, "I can stop working for you; if it will make things easier for you."

"You will do no such thing. There's no harm in two people expressing their feelings."

"I'm so sorry, Miss Annie. This will do nothing but cause trouble, and I don't like trouble."

"You're fine, dear. Besides, we haven't done anything...yet," she said as she leaned in to kiss Josiah.

Their passion from years before picked up where it had left

off. He returned her kisses as he pulled her closer to him until he fell flat against the ground. On top of him, Annie grabbed hold of Josiah's face with both hands as she ground her body against his.

For the first few minutes, Josiah had his hands stretched out beside him; unsure of what to do with them. Annie released her lips from his and lifted herself to straddle his groin. Her skirt, now balled up around her waist, was raised above her head and thrown to the ground, leaving only her top and camisole. Reaching behind her to grab Josiah's lust, her purse throbbed in ecstasy when she wrapped her hand around it. Its firmness sent spasms through her as she reached for both his hands and pressed them against her breasts. Massaging them, Josiah wanted more from her and began to tenderly remove her top and camisole. He lifted himself from the ground and met her breasts with his mouth. Encircling them with his tongue, Josiah freed his hands so he could unfasten his pants and pull them down below his waist to expose him to her cavern. Annie, consumed with the love buried deep within her, slid her finger between her legs to feel the moisture brought on by Josiah. She moaned, finding bliss in her own space, and, seconds later, Josiah entered her, jolting the cavern's walls with strokes of pleasure.

❂❂❂

The carriage returned to the house shortly after sunset, and Josiah stopped in front of the house as he normally did. Sitting still for a moment, Annie recalled the events of the afternoon and wondered how she was going to go about the rest of the day. Josiah got down from his seat to open the door for her but found it increasingly difficult to look at her in the face—something he had always been able to do.

As she emerged from the coach, Annie noticed Josiah staring at the ground in front of her. "What's wrong, Josiah?"

"Nothing, ma'am," he said as he helped her down off the step.

Puzzled by Josiah's demeanor, Annie asked, "Is everything alright?"

"It will be," he said softly, escorting her up the walk. When they got to the door, he looked out toward the barn and did not see light from the fire John Otis usually kept burning. Josiah wanted so badly to kiss Annie but was not willing to take that chance. "Good night, ma'am."

Deeply affected by Josiah's actions, Annie asked, "Will I see you tomorrow?"

Unable to look her in the face, Josiah replied, "Yes, ma'am; if you want to."

Drawing close enough to Josiah to feel his breath against her neck, she professed, "Wanting to see you is something I can control, and I can choose whether or not it happens. But needing to see you is something I cannot control, and it is something I have no choice but to do. My heart tells me that I need to see you."

"Out of the overflow of the heart, the mouth speaks," Josiah whispered.

"So true, my love, so true." Annie sighed as she cupped his chin with her soft hands and then disappeared into the threshold of the house.

❁❁❁

Late in the morning, right before the sun peaked noon, Annie was in the kitchen preparing teacakes for her tea with Lisbeth when she heard the splitting of wood in the backyard. She walked over to the window and saw Josiah, who was shirtless, chopping wood for the stove. His muscles jerking every time he swung the ax, Josiah's stern facial expression was one of determination. Closing her eyes, she remembered the many times they had walked through the meadow and the orchard and the peace she felt when she was with him. She expected herself to flutter with apprehension, for she never knew if anyone would ever see them and report back to Royce. However, she did not care, and she knew Josiah, in a big way, felt the same way. Annie poured a glass of cool water, picked up a freshly, cleaned towel, and went out the back door.

"Cool drink?" she asked softly as she lifted the glass to Josiah's face.

Josiah, who was in the middle of a swing, stopped himself when he saw his beautiful Annie standing there. "Why, yes, ma'am. That's mighty kind of you."

"Much obliged." She smiled. "I brought a towel for you, too, so you can wipe yourself off."

"Thank you, Miss Annie." He smiled in return. It was the middle of the day, and the plantation was busy. With servants bustling about, he kept his manners about him; even though it drove him mad. "You're getting ready for your tea with Miss Lisbeth, I suppose?"

Like a little ole school girl, Annie returned, "Yes, I am. The teacakes are about ready. Want one?"

"No, ma'am. I want to get back to chopping this wood so you all can have wood for the house. Don't seem like you got enough men folk working around here."

Annie commented, "No, we don't, but we get by pretty fine with what we have." Taken by his prowess and immeasurable love for her, Annie looked around to see if anyone was looking. "You know, Josiah, I really enjoyed yesterday. I feel like we connected in some way. You're a passionate man."

Slurping the last of his water, Josiah said, "I could maybe agree with you, but I don't think we should be talking about this out here."

As she took the glass he handed to her, she agreed, "You're right. I mustn't bring it up out here. I'm going to return to the kitchen. Here's a towel for you to keep out here." Annie turned and went back into the house.

❋❋❋

Unusually late, Lisbeth, instead of coming by foot as she normally did, arrived at Annie's in a carriage busting at its seams with suitcases. Annie gingerly stepped off the back porch and walked hurriedly down the path to greet her. The driver never exited his seat as Lisbeth sat still in hers. "Why, Lisbeth, what on earth is going on? You brought all this just so we could have tea?" she joked.

Lisbeth, fumbling through her travel satchel, answered tersely, "I'm leaving this place. There ain't nothing here for me any more."

Annie placed her hands on the edge of the carriage window, extending one of them inside the carriage to grab hold of Lisbeth's hand. "Tell me, please. What has happened?" Annie pleaded.

"I don't like my life here any longer. I'm headed to Virginny, where my mother is."

"What about your husband? You can't leave him like this."

"Watch me," she said emphatically.

Everything was happening so fast, and Annie was heartbroken that Lisbeth had already made up her mind to leave without at least discussing it with anyone. "Will is going to be hurt behind you leaving so suddenly."

In an instant, Lisbeth angrily turned to Annie and looked her square in the eye. "We should have never married."

Annie was used to hearing unkind words from Lisbeth, but this caught her off guard. "What an awful thing to say, Lisbeth. That man loves you."

"You think so? Well, why don't you ask that young nigger that I found him ramming up the ass in our bed? Is that love, Annie? Tell me, is that love?" she jeered.

Stepping away from the carriage and covering her mouth in disbelief, Annie said, "Oh, my god, Lisbeth. I don't know what to say."

"There ain't nothing to say. I will not stay around here to be humiliated by an ol' Southern sissy who likes splitting the asses of his niggers." Finally, she stumbled upon what she had been digging for in her bag. "Oh, here it is. I brought this for you," she said pleasantly as she handed Annie an ornately decorated gold trinket box.

"What's this?"

"It's from Germany, and it belonged to my father's whore. She gave it to me as a gift as some sort of peace offering, and, quite honestly, I never wanted the old thing in the first place. Ol' cunt had the nerve to tell me that I was the only piece of white trash she knew would appreciate it."

Quietly offended, Annie asked, "And you're giving it to me?"

"Why, yes, Annie, I am," she said sarcastically. "When you look at it, think of how fucked up life can really be sometimes."

"Lisbeth, what am I going to do without you? What about our afternoon tea?" she cried.

"Annie, you don't get it, do you? You have everything you've ever wanted, and, if you are truly the friend you say you are, then you should want the same for me." Without waiting to see if her best friend had anything else to say, Lisbeth tapped the side of the coach, signaling the driver that she was ready to leave.

8

Although he was largely respected by members of the military community, Royce Smith was considered the White man's agitator. He ruffled feathers from one side of town to the other with his political opinions. Greatly against President Jackson, Royce proudly announced his affiliation with the Whig party in the early spring of 1835, refusing to support the candidate from the political party of his peers. By that September, his affairs diverted him to Bibb County where he spent a great deal of his time away from home. Then, in November of the same year, he led a group of sympathizers from Macon and attempted to organize a company to go to Texas and help them fight a war with the Mexicans. Royce committed over three thousand dollars of his own money to cover the expenses of the trip. Appointed commander of the company, Royce resigned his commission with the United States Army to become a volunteer for the cause of liberty.

Shortly thereafter, Commander Royce Smith left for Texas by way of Columbus, Georgia where they joined the Columbus Company. From there, they went on to Montgomery. With him, he took Maynard, Susie's husband, and John Otis to shoe the horses for the company. Back then, it was considered an honor to be asked to travel with your master. It didn't matter that you'd be away from your family for long stretches of time, nor did it matter that you'd have twenty or thirty masters instead of one. Even though John Otis and Maynard were Royce's favorites, they had never liked one another because Maynard ended up with Susie when it was actually John Otis that wanted and loved her. You see, that was Royce's fault. Being the evil, conniving snake that he was, Royce picked on the weak, male slaves. John Otis was about the color of the top of an acorn and had all the respect of the slaves around his quarters because he was not afraid to talk to back to Royce, or to any other White man. If he got a beating for it, then he took it like an ox and went on back to work out in the fields. He was a crazy nigger who would likely kill a man with his bare hands if he had to. A couple of times he and Maynard fought out in the yard to show off in front of Susie, but she wasn't the least bit moved by all of the attention.

❁❁❁

Before the company could leave Alabama, Maynard had made up in his mind that he could not and would not be able to provide loyalty to Royce and to the other members of the company. His work was more grueling than what he had experienced back at the plantation, and, at the root of it all, he missed his Susie. Maynard had a good mind and put it to good use when he marked trees along their trail with a piece of coal. He was determined to find his way back home.

When it was discovered that Maynard had escaped, Royce, devoted to the revolution in Texas, chose not to go after him but relied on the efforts of the slave patrols to catch him. All along the Georgia-Alabama line, slave patrols infested the woods and brush to find runaways. Royce was sure Maynard would never make it back home alive. John Otis had been asked to join him, but refused, saying that he wanted to earn his freedom. Late one evening, after all the other soldiers had gone to bed, John Otis was standing over the fire to thaw his hands after having washed the dinner pots and pans. None of the niggers were allowed to be around the fire at the same time as the whites unless they were serving them food.

Minutes later, Royce emerged from his tent with a blanket tightly wrapped around him. "It's cold as hell in there," he scoffed. "Shoot, I'd start a fire in there, if I didn't think I'd set myself ablaze."

John Otis stepped aside to allow Royce room to get to the flames. "Herh, ya go, suh. You kin git right herh whar itz nice and woam."

Never one to exchange pleasantries with his niggers, Royce stepped in front of John Otis and took a seat on an upside-down pail. "Boy, you can come on over here and sit down on the ground to get yourself warm 'cause if you freeze to death here I won't have nobody to shoe my horses."

"Yessuh," John Otis responded.

❂❂❂

While several silent minutes passed between them, John Otis considered how he would pose his request for freedom. He was holding information no one else knew and was certain it was something Royce wanted to know. "Suh?" he asked as the shadow of the flames bounced against the earth.

"What you want, boy?" Royce snapped.

"Itz 'bout mah freedom, suh. I wuz wondrin' if-n I jes talk te ya 'bout sum thangs you might lemme go wins us gits bak te Joe-gee."

Royce loved his nigger snitches. During the routine, he would promise them their freedom and then make then pour their souls out to him. By the end of the conversation, he had convinced them that the best place for them was his plantation. To seal the deal, he would tell them they could have a small piece of land after he died.

"I'm listening." He chuckled, stuffing a wad of tobacco into his left side of his jaw.

"A lil' wiles bak you knowed you tells me te aw-ways go wid Josiah wins he takes the missus 'roun."

"Yes, I did," he said, chewing.

"An-uh, I'se wus doin' dat til one day, an-uh, deys go widout me."

"So what, John Otis? Miss Annie mighta been in a hurry."

John Otis began fidgeting and could not find anything to do with his hands, so he started throwing more wood into the fire. "Yessuh, uh, but dey comes bak, and Josiah walks de missus te da do' and den, suh, I seent dem do thangs not propah fa a nigger and missus te do."

Glaring into the fire without words for what he had heard, Royce spat into the ground. "Boy, where was you when all this was going on?"

"I wus out in da barn, suh, waitin' on dem te git bak so I'se could shoe da horses."

Royce was furious but refused to let it show. Again, he spat on the ground, barely missing John Otis. His feeling was that a nigger would say anything to get his freedom, but he would have to be a damn fool to go this far. "Is that all, boy?"

"Wells, no massa. Deys bin gwone way a few udder times widout me."

It seemed real hard to separate the fire in Royce's eyes from the blaze on the ground. He sat there, stone-faced, and then spewed venomous words to John Otis. "Nigger, let me tell you something I don't ever want you to forget. You don't talk about my wife like that. If I ever hear such a cockamamie story again, I'll kill you on the spot 'cause I'll know you done run off at the mouth to somebody."

John Otis, the big, bad nigger that he was, got chopped down—and, for what it was worth, he had also managed to sign his own death papers.

❂❂❂

Several days before Annie's twentieth birthday, Litton Few suffered a massive stroke, and the doctor told Risella he did not have much time to live. After almost ten years of living in the cabin with Josiah, Risella moved back into the house to take care of her husband in his final days. She bathed him, read to him, and fed him to try to make up for the years she had missed with him. Despite the reason they were apart, Litton enjoyed having her back in his life. At night, she held him close to her with hopes of him realizing that her love for him had never gone away. In the afternoons, Risella brought him tea and peach teacakes. While his words were mildly slurred, his mind was pretty much intact. He was still ornery but seemed to have let up a bit when it came to his lack of compassion toward Josiah.

Risella, one cool, lazy Saturday afternoon before tea, sat down next to her husband as he relaxed in his rose garden. "Litton, are you up to talking for a minute?"

"Sure, darling."

"It's about Josiah."

Conversations about Josiah had been few and far between, but Risella was determined to live up to her promise to Hattie. Litton's mood about everything was he was too old and too sick to give a damn about much of anything, so his wife took advantage of it. "What about him?"

"You know I've been around him most of his life, and he doesn't fit in around here anymore. He's not a slave or a servant."

"Isn't he still driving for Annie?"

"Yes, he is, but that is because he wants to. He has no business over there. If Royce finds out he can read and write, then you know what's likely to happen. He's a smart young man and should really be somewhere other than this dreadful place. Besides, I…"

Frowning slightly, Litton said, "I know, you promised his mother, and you don't want to break that promise." Clearing his throat, Litton asked, "What do you want, Risella? I don't really have anything to offer to him."

"You can give him his freedom," she said.

"How can I give freedom to someone who doesn't want to be free? Hell, he's the one who asked to be over at Royce and Annie's place."

"In all his years, he has never talked about being given his freedom, nor has he ever tried to take it. Considering the circumstances, he should be rewarded for that."

Litton poked out his lip and turned it toward the sky. Despite his learned behavior toward Negroes, he knew Risella was right. Josiah had been the ideal son—should he have been white—and he had never had any problems out of him. Still haunted by the day Quincy was killed, Litton realized it was time for him to do what was best.

"June is in Massachusetts and maybe she has a place for him there. They treat the Negroes real well up there."

That was what Risella had been counting on. "I will write a letter and get it on its way."

It would take a few months to get a response from June, and that was all the time Risella needed. There was no telling when Royce was going to be back, so she knew she had to move quickly.

Litton had no idea that his wife had a motive behind her request, and he would die several days later not knowing Annie was carrying his grandchild.

❖❖❖

Once Miss Lisbeth left, Susie and Ina went back to work in the main house, and they saw Annie's belly getting bigger and bigger every day but dared not utter a word about it. They merely made it their purpose to look after her and fetch whatever she needed. The day Risella found out Annie was with child, she immediately knew the child belonged to Josiah.

"Do you realize what you've done?" she scolded tearfully.

Annie wept and pleaded with her mother, "Please, Mama, don't be upset with me."

Angrily, Risella reproached, "You're no different than your father. He put the nails in Quincy's coffin, and you have done the same for Josiah. He's a good man, and he's been foolish enough to let you ruin that."

"It was not his fault. I did it. For years, he had pushed me away, but things simply got out of hand that day. Josiah understands me."

"What about your husband, Annie?"

"Royce does not love me for me. He loves me for how I make him look when his friends come around."

Risella retorted, "How the hell do you think this is going to make him look now? Those people will send a lynch mob here for that boy."

"You've got to help him, Mama. You've got to help him. Please, please, if you have never done anything else to prove you love me, please do this."

Seeing how distraught Annie was, Risella tried to comfort her. "How many times has this happened?"

"Only once, but..."

"But nothing. If you want me to fix this, you will have to stay away from him. No one can ever know what has happened."

To protect Annie, Risella moved in to receive visitors, particularly the wives of Royce's friends, telling them Annie was away visiting family

The next conversation Risella had was with Josiah. She recognized he had been distant with her and remained mostly to himself. While Annie spoke freely of her relationship with him, Josiah kept his feelings to himself. Later, on the same day that she had spoken to Annie, she found him in the orchard. Risella sat down next to him, sighed, and reached for his hand. His grasp was firm as he held her hand as tight as he could.

"When you were a little boy, you used to hold my hand like this whenever you were scared. Do you remember that?"

"Yes, ma'am, I do," he said affectionately. "I knew you would protect me from things."

Tapping the back of his hand with her other hand, she comforted, "You need to know that nothing's changed. We're going to get through this."

Josiah, who usually walked proud with his head held high, lowered his head in disgrace. "I love Miss Annie, ma'am," he said. "I never meant her any harm."

"I know you didn't, dear. It's going to be alright. I promise."

❂❂❂

Close to the beginning of March, Susie was in the backyard doing laundry when she looked up and saw Maynard standing by a tree in the distance. His clothes were torn and dirty, and, as much as she wanted to run to him, she pretended not to see him because there were no signs of Royce or John Otis. It was comfort enough to see that he was still alive and back in Georgia. After completing her chores, Susie went out to the quarters, hoping that she'd find Maynard, but was disappointed when she got there and he was nowhere to be found. She asked a few of the others if they had seen him, and they wondered if Susie had started losing her mind. Maynard, as far as they knew, was with Royce. The next morning, when she went out to the well to get water, she saw Maynard again standing beside a tree waving for her to come to him.

"T'nigh, meet me whar da plantation drops from da urth," he whispered in her ear as they embraced.

There was only one spot on the plantation where the earth seemed to drop off, and it was beyond the meadow that actually sat between Fews Grove and Royce's place. Right at the edge, boulders were stacked one on top of the other and sewn together by roots and moss. To get to the bottom, there was a seven-foot leap to the sandy bank of the river. It was a good way to escape to freedom, if you thought you could survive the jump. Susie arrived at the place where Maynard had told her to meet him, and, as promised, he was waiting for her.

"Anybody see ya?"

"No, dey din't."

"I'se needs ya te take mah hand an comes wid me."

Susie extended her hand, and Maynard led her to a huge crevice just to the side of the boulders. He stepped down first and then reached for her. She heard the water rushing beneath them and hesitated slightly.

"Itz aw'right, Susie. Come on."

"Wutz dis, Maynard? Whar you takin' me?"

"To freedum."

Susie followed Maynard, and as darkness descended, she relied on him to guide her the rest of the way. Through vines and roots, Maynard stepped into a hole in the side of the earth.

"Dis is home, Susie."

"Wut?" She smiled in awe.

"I'se built dis fa us. I'se bin bak from Texie for a good whiles."

Susie, while glad she was finally back with her husband, asked, "You runt away?"

"I'se did. Massa ain't even comes lookin' fa me. Down herh, us ain't got no massa no mo'."

"I dunno 'bout dis, Maynard. If'n he comes bak and fines you, he..."

The only way he could quiet her was to put his lips against hers. With tongues twisted and memories recollected, Maynard brought himself back from the places he had traveled to get back home and from the fear deep within him that one day he would be punished for running away in the first place.

As Susie lay in his arms, she told him about all the things that had happened while he had been gone. "I'se wurd 'bout missus. She looked lak she 'bout te buss but dat baby ain't near 'bout ready te come out yet."

Maynard, still holding Susie, asked curiously, "Da missus 'bout te haf a baby?"

"Yez. Looked lak any dey nah. You s'pose da war be ovah fo den?"

"I'se dunno, Susie. I ne'er even got dat far wid dem."

"Oh, well, I'se glad you home wid me nah."

While Susie slept, Maynard revisited in his mind the conversation between him and John Otis when he was planning on running away. Maynard had worked through his plans and had only been waiting for the perfect opportunity to come. John Otis, however, told him that he had his own plan for obtaining his freedom. He was asked to share it but refused, saying it was something only one nigger could afford to know. Then one evening, as they marched toward Montgomery, Maynard had overheard Royce telling one of the other lieutenants that Miss Annie wanted to wait until after he returned from the war to begin having children. To keep her from being uncomfortable, he wanted to make sure that he had sold off all the children he had made with his slaves, and that would be the first thing he did when he returned from the war.

By the time the bell in the fields sounded, Susie was back at the main house in place as if nothing in her life had changed. Maynard had furnished the cave with a table, two chairs and a bed made of hay and chicken feathers. Susie had gotten some candles from Ina and taken them to the place she now called home. After several weeks of watching Susie come and go, Risella finally asked her where she went at night because one evening they had come looking for her in the cabin, and she was not there. They had noticed most of her belongings were gone.

"Now, Susie, you should know you all can trust me around here."

"Yessum, miss, I knows," she said. She then proceeded to tell Risella about her home in the side of the earth and the fact that Maynard had escaped and had built them a cave to live in.

"Where's this place?"

"Itz at ovah whar it lookt lak itz da edge of the earth on da udder side of the meadah."

❋❋❋

That evening Risella went into to Annie's room to check on her because she had not been up most of the day. The drapes were still closed, and Annie was sleeping. Just as she was about to touch Annie's forehead, Ina walked in. "Ina, how has Miss Annie been today? Why is the room so dark?"

"Miss Annie, ma'am, she won't derrin' too good and askt fo us te send fo da dokter."

"What? You did what?" she shrieked. It was the only moment in her entire life that she had ever raised her voice at a slave. "You silly girl; please tell me you didn't do that."

Confused as to why she would not have wanted her to help Miss Annie feel better, Ina said, "She wus bleedin', ma'am. You wus gone off, and us din't know wut else te do."

"Did he come?"

"Yez, he did. Seh he din't even knowed Miss Annie wus carryin' no baby. Gives hue a li'l sumthin' te make hur feel bettah. Wanted te know if Massa Royce knowed sens off at da war."

Frantically, Risella said, "Oh, my sweet Jesus. We're going to have to get her out of here." Pacing the floor, it did not take her long to figure out what to do. "Go fetch Josiah, and tell him to hurry. Tell him to bring the carriage."

"Yessum, ma'am."

Risella ran downstairs and found Susie in the kitchen preparing supper. "Susie, we will be taking Miss Annie out to that cave of yours for a spell. There will not be any fuss about it. If anyone comes by here to call on her, she's still away visiting family."

"Yessum, ma'am."

"Oh, and if by chance you or anybody else catches word of Massa Royce's return, you get to me as quick as you can."

"Yessum, ma'am."

❈❈❈

Josiah got to the house within the hour and was led to Miss Annie's bedroom where he took her into his arms and carried her to the carriage. Susie sat next to him in the driver's seat and showed him how to get to the cave. When they arrived at the boulders, Maynard was waiting for them with a lantern to guide them through the darkness to the cave's entrance.

Nestled against Josiah's shoulder, Annie whispered to him, "I'm so sorry."

"Nothing to be sorry about," he replied. "We're going to be fine."

His main focus was on getting her to a place where she could rest. Risella had packed sheets, towels, fresh clothes for Annie, and a small jar of whiskey. She also brought the silk blankets that Penny had made for Annie and Josiah when they were babies. Once inside, Annie was immediately put to bed but quickly began complaining about the pain in her belly. Risella poured Annie a small glass of whiskey and instructed her to drink it. With Ina and Susie by her side, Risella asked Josiah and Maynard to wait outside and keep watch.

A very short time afterwards, Annie gave birth to a little girl she named Amelia. "Mama, the pain is coming back again. This time it's worse," she moaned as she passed the baby to Ina.

Risella lifted Annie's dress and saw that her belly was still firm. "It can't be," she said as she pressed gently against the bump.

Annie's shrill sent her into a twilight sleep as Ina and Susie stood there in shock. Nature took over, and another baby came out, but it did not make a sound. Risella quickly wrapped it in a blanket and took it outside where she held it close to her and forced life into him by pushing short breaths into his mouth.

Josiah walked over to her and asked, "Can I..." Before he could finish his sentence, Risella handed him the baby wrapped in swaddling.

"Here is your son," she said tearfully. "He's going to be fine. God's just taking His time with him; that's all."

Holding him and now pushing his breaths into his tiny mouth, Josiah rubbed the baby's chest. "Welcome, my son, welcome," he said joyfully. Then there came a sudden cry from his arms, and Josiah's eyes warmed with tears as held the baby tightly.

"You have a daughter, too, Josiah. Her name is Amelia."

❂❂❂

Two days after the births, Risella asked Josiah to take her back to the house. For most of the ride, she was speechless. When they got to what equaled the middle of nowhere, she told him to stop the carriage. "Josiah, we should get out here."

"Yes, ma'am."

Clutching his arm, Risella walked with him a few yards from the carriage where she pulled out a letter. "Before Litton died, I asked him for your freedom."

Under the impression he had always been free, he questioned, "Ma'am?"

"This letter I have here in my hand is from June, Litton's sister who lives in Massachusetts, and she said you can come to live with her."

"And leave Annie and my children?"

Not surprised by his reaction, Risella said, "You know you can't stay here. You're a dead man, and you know that."

Josiah knew Risella was right. If word got out he'd ever been with Annie in a natural way, he would be killed. Reluctantly, he asked, "So what am I supposed to do?"

"I will accompany you to Massachusetts to make the journey easier for you, and you will have to take your son."

"What?"

"A male child with pale white skin, blue-eyes and black wavy hair can't stay on this plantation. At least not right now. It's for his and your own good."

"What am I to do about Annie and Amelia?"

"I've spoken to Annie about everything, and she has no choice but to be fine with it. Ina and Susie will look after them until Annie gets better. We received word last night the war in Texas is over, and Royce and his company are on the way home."

"What about Amelia?"

"Ina will take care of her out in the cave, and I'm sure Annie will make a way to be with her when possible. In the meantime, once you drop me off, you need to pack your things and be ready to leave at sunrise."

"Yes, ma'am." Walking back to the carriage, Josiah asked, "Did she name him yet?"

"Yes, she did. His name is Quincy Josiah."

❂❂❂

In the wee hours of the first Sunday morning of June, Annie awakened to the sound of the rumbling of horses' hooves. She got up from her bed, went to the window and saw that Royce and his company had come home.

"Where's my wife?" he asked loudly as he dismounted his horse. Several members of his company were with him to have one last meal with their commander before they returned to their respective homes.

"Walcum, Massa Royce," the servants offered one right after the other.

Without properly acknowledging them, he demanded, "Get out to the kitchen and prepare a meal of jambalaya, rice and beans, and pork for my soldiers. They have fought a powerful war against the Mexicans and deserve to be rewarded with a good home-cooked meal."

"Yessum," they replied, scurrying off in various directions of the house.

"Where's my wife, damnit?"

Susie, on her way to the garden to get fresh vegetables, answered, "She still sleepin', suh."

Royce made a dash for the upstairs.

❂❂❂

Annie, still peering out the window, watched Royce's men, who were filled with lust and malice, take off toward the quarters to find themselves some unsuspecting female slaves to have their way with. Only one or two of them remained behind. Now that Royce was home, she could no longer protect the slaves from any type of cruelty. Her body nearly mended, Annie walked toward the door to greet Royce with the slightest bit of warmth and compassion she could find. Her spirit had been broken since the day Josiah and her son left, and she did not even have her mother to visit with. The single piece of joy she had was her daily walk to the edge of the plantation to visit Amelia. With Royce back, she was going to have to be careful about her comings and goings because he did not miss a thing. As his footsteps hurried across the wooden floor toward his bedroom door, Annie prepared herself for his embrace.

Royce burst into the room and found Annie sitting on the bed. "There you are!" he said excitedly. "Oh, how I have missed you!"

"Oh, my love, I have missed you even more!" she whimpered. Her tears came not from his presence but from the absence of love she had for him. Royce wasted no time reaching for Annie and rushed through his motions in order to get himself into her. Pounding her like a hammer against petrified wood, Royce's face lacked passion, for he was merely in the moment for his own satisfaction. Annie, grasping the sides of the bed to balance herself, received him with no pleasure and gave only when asked.

9

In 1858, Mother had reached the age of forty-two years and had been blessed enough to have been able to raise me in the cave just beyond the meadow without Royce discovering it. Despite laws passed in Georgia prohibiting blacks from knowing how to read and write, Annie had not only taught me how to read and write but how to cook and clean. I was taught the most formal English, which did not include the use of contractions or local dialect when writing or talking with others. I even taught Susie, Ina and Maynard—who over the years had two children born free—how to read and write as well.

As I grew into adulthood, Mother realized it was important for me to know who I was and to also know that my life could be taken from me in an instant if anyone discovered who I was. I had grown into a lovely, young woman with piercing blue eyes like my mother and had straight, black hair that waved when it was hit with water. My nose was slightly large and rounded at its tip, and my cheekbones were high like Mother's were. I had been given a somewhat privileged life, although it was mostly spent in a dwelling with little to no light, no windows or real furniture. It was crowded at times, but I had no complaints.

"My love, you need to know there is more to this world than what Susie, Ina, Maynard and I have provided for you here."

"Yes, Mother. You have told me that before."

"No, I told you only what your youthful innocence could handle. You're a woman now, and things are different," she said as she reached for a bag she had often kept in the corner of the cave. "I have raised you in darkness all these years, and you must now be prepared to live in the light." In the bag, she pulled out a gold trinket box and three silk blankets.

"I don't understand."

Mother calmly explained, "In here, with your family, you are the joy of our lives; making us smile and laugh as we watch you grow. In here, you are free to do whatever you want. I've kept you hidden from the cruelty that Susie and Ina have experienced every single day of their lives. Maynard hides here because if my husband finds him, he will kill him for having escaped many years ago."

Curiously, I asked, "If your husband is my father, then why am I hidden out here and why does he not want anything to do with me; since you say I bring only joy to you all?"

"That's just it, Amelia, dear. My husband is not your father. He's the owner of Susie, Ina, Maynard and the other slaves on this plantation."

"Since you are his wife, does that make you a slave owner, too?"

"In theory, it does, but in reality it does not. Although I was raised around it, I do not believe in slavery, and I do not wish to have you a part of it either; if I have anything to do with it."

As Mother educated me on how life was outside the cave, I could not help but ask about my father. "Where is he then, Mother? Where is my father?"

"In Massachusetts." Then, without warning, her mood changed, and she directed her attention to the items she had held in the bag. "This trinket box belonged to my very best friend, and she gave it to me before she left to go up North. This large blanket belonged to her as well, and she left it for me, too. These other ones belonged to me and your father and were made by your grandmother. All of these things are heirlooms, and, should anything happen to me, the items are to be given to you. Know that, if you get them from someone else other than me in this lifetime, then I am no more."

The thought of something happening to Mother was preposterous, and I erased her statements from my conscience. "Will I ever get to meet him, my father?"

Looking around the room at Ina and Susie as if to get their approval for what she was to say next, she replied, "Your father is a Negro, and for his safety, it is best he never return to Georgia. While he was never enslaved, the love he and I had for one another can still cost the both of you your lives. Despite what anyone else tells you, remember that you are not a slave because your mother was never a slave. However, if it becomes a matter of life or death for you, then show what will save your life."

At that moment, Ina, seeing Mother's anguish with discussing such things, said, "Miss Millie, lets missus be. Hur kin talks wid ya lader 'bout dis." And that she did. For weeks, Mother told me about where I had come from and where I could likely find my family; if I needed to. Most importantly she explained to me how I was to conduct myself amongst others should I ever happen to leave my surroundings. I was the one thing whites feared the most—a Negro who could read, write, and had never spent a day in slavery. She also told me how awful of a man she was married to and how he despised Negroes.

"Should my husband ever come here for you, then you run—

run like the devil is trying to catch up to you and don't look back," she warned.

During the day while Mother was up at the main house, Susie, Ina, and Maynard taught me how to speak as they did and how to act as they did when they were around Royce and other whites. I did not like it one bit, but it was for my own good. They called me Millie for short sometimes, and encouraged me to use it as my name when on the outside. Maynard, believing his survival skills would help me one day, told me how he had learned to survive in the cave for so long. As we stood looking at the water rushing below, he told me that if I ever had to jump, to make sure I did not land flat on my feet because it would break the bones in my legs. "If-n you jumps an lans lak a cat, the sand'll ketch ya. Don't forgit dat."

◉◉◉

Toward the end of January of 1859, Royce was in town conducting his affairs relating to his cotton crops when he ran into the good doctor that once lived down the road from him. "Good day, Doctor Ogden. I haven't seen you in years."

"Well, that's a good thing, I guess. Means you and your family been taking care of yourselves." He chuckled. "I opened a practice in town where there were more sick people. You all didn't keep me busy enough."

Boasting of his health, Royce added, "Yes, we do pretty good for an ol' married couple. Nothing more than a cold every now and again."

"Good, good. How's that child of yours? Oughta be about twenty or so, give or take a year or two."

While the look on his face did not change, the tone of his voice was that of disbelief and confusion. "What did you say, Doc? My hearing is a little weak on one side."

"The last time I was out at your place, Miss Annie was about to give birth. It was around the time you were down in Texas."

"Oh, right, right." Royce's voice had changed from warm and friendly to angry and vengeful.

"She still had a little while to go when I got there so I went back home. I came back, but she wasn't there. Place looked like a ghost town. Was it a girl or boy?"

"The whole family's fine. I must get on my way, Doctor Ogden. I'm late for a meeting.

"Carry on," the doctor said cheerfully. "Tell Miss Annie I said hello."

No force of nature could match the thunder of Royce's horse's hooves as they pounded the earth, creating a trail of dust back to the plantation. John Otis, who had been hanged by members of Royce's company for his blatant disobedience and disrespect, had tried twice to tell his master of his wife's infidelity with a nigger. Royce had no reason at all to believe him but had given credence to the notice in his dreams and sometimes found himself intertwined in nightmares from which he could not awaken.

❁❁❁

Royce arrived at the house to find Mother in the kitchen with Susie preparing supper. Wordlessly, he approached her and slapped her in the face with all his might, and, before she could hit the floor, he slapped her again. Repeatedly, the blows came from his fists, his hands, and his feet. "How dare you humiliate me this way! You whore! You nigger-loving whore!" As blood ran from Mother's nose and mouth, Susie tried to help her get to her feet, but each time Royce kicked her to back to the ground. "You been helping her, nigger? Have you?" he screamed.

Susie, indebted to Mother for all she had done for her and Maynard, did not utter a word.

"With my bare hands, nigger, I will kill you if you don't answer me when I ask you a question."

Annie knew she should not have expected anything less from her husband. "Please, Royce," she mumbled. "Leave her out of this." Holding her stomach, Mother rose to her feet and requested that Susie leave her and her husband alone. For Susie, that was the signal.

"Where is it? Where is the bastard, Annie?" he asked as he slapped her yet again. "You can't give me a child, but you had one with a nigger?"

"Royce, if you would hold on," she begged as she continued swallowing gulps of her own blood.

"Hold on? What the fuck do I hold on for? You had a child with that nigger I let come here and look after you. Where is he?"

Mother, with what fire she could muster, exclaimed, "He is not here, Royce. He's long gone from this place."

Grasping her by her upper arms, he began shaking her until she managed to pull away from him. Helplessly, he fought tears as he tried to bear the burden of knowing his wife had kept this secret for over twenty years "All these years, you have lied to me. How could you, Annie, how could you?"

Weeping only for what was to come of me and not for any injustice done to her husband, Annie responded, "I have loved another man all my life, Royce, and, yes, it was Josiah. While you may want me to be sorry for it, I shall not be."

Pulling his Gunnison revolver from its holster and pointing it in the middle of her forehead, he commanded, "You will take me to this child, and you will do it now."

❁❁❁

The night had begun to push daylight from the sky as Mother walked to the edge of the plantation for what could be the last time. Susie had gone before her to warn everyone of what had happened and to get everyone out of the cave, especially me. She was heartbroken when she discovered I had gone out for my evening walk. Only Ina and Maynard knew what path I always took so they set out, with the bag of heirlooms, to find me. Royce, marching behind my mother with the revolver sticking in her back, sniveled like a spoiled brat as he continued to taunt Mother with horrible names. While walking through the woods and then the meadow, he noticed the amount of trouble she had gone through to keep this secret.

When they got to where the boulders were stacked one on top of the other, Mother stopped, turned to Royce and pleaded, "Please do not hurt my daughter. She has done nothing to you and does not deserve to be punished. This is all my fault." She recalled the day she had said those same words to her mother.

"Bitch, if you don't take me to her, I will blow your head off. It's just that simple." Mother climbed down into the crevice and was pleased to find the cave empty. Royce followed her inside and only grew angrier when he realized someone knew he was coming. "That ole nigger of mine came down here and warned

I was coming." Then, as Mother walked deeper into the cave to make sure the bag was indeed gone, Royce fired twice upon her and exited the cave.

❁❁❁

"Did you hear that?" I cried out to Ina and Maynard, leading them to back to the cave with Mother's bag of heirlooms tossed over my shoulder. They had found me as I was on my way back home and alerted me that Royce had discovered my existence. I asked where Susie was, and they told me she was hiding in the brush to look after Mother; in case things went horribly wrong.

"Yessum, Miss Millie. Dat sound lak gunshots."

"We have to hurry," I said hastily.

Maynard lunged for me, grabbing me by the arm, and said, "Miss Millie, please wait. If-n you goes in dare nah, Massa gon killz ya, and Miss Annie ain't want dat fo ya. He is not a nice man."

"Uncle Maynard, I'm not going to leave my mother in there to die. I simply cannot do that."

Ina, who had taken care of me since I was a baby, came to me and said, "Miss Millie, dar's nethin' you kin do fa her. Susie wus leff behind to look afta hur."

"No!" I screamed. "I have to go back to her."

"Shhh," Maynard hushed to us. "Sumbody comin'."

I, dressed in a black cloak given to me by my mother, pulled the hood over my head, squatted into the brush and remained still. Ina and Maynard stood as still as the trees that surrounded us.

A dark image passed by us while we stood motionless. We could hear his hesitant footsteps and heavy panting. As soon as he was out of sight, we moved on toward the cave. Our steps became quicker as we got closer. Seeing Susie standing just beyond the boulders, Maynard and Ina rushed to her to make sure she was alright. "Wut 'bout Miss Annie? Us hurd gunshots, and…"

"Have you seen Mother?" I asked frantically.

"No, miss, I wus jes 'bout te go in dare and see 'bout hur."

Maynard climbed down into the crevice first, and then helped Ina and Susie down. Just as he reached for my hand, a man's voice yelled to me, "Wait right there."

My eyes met Maynard's to say good-bye, for I was not willing to give him up. "Go," I whispered. "I will be fine." He had been a free man for as long as I had breath in me, and I refused to let him sacrifice that. I watched him and the others disappear into the darkness.

"You turn around real slow, if you know what's good for you," the man's voice ordered.

Standing atop the boulders, I embraced my life for all that it had been. I remembered my mother and the richness of the love she had surrounded me with all my life. I thought about the family I had waiting for me should I make it to glory, but I, too, thought about the ones I had waiting on this earth for me right now. The passion between my parents had brought me into this world, and it was the passion that I had for life that would take me to where I was to go next. I turned around with my hood partially covering my eyes as I laid eyes on the man that had tried to hold my mother's passion hostage. He was the first White man I had ever seen, and I was not sure if he would be the last.

Pulling my hood back and still holding on to Mother's heirlooms, I revealed to him my beauty, for I was the spitting image of both my mother and father. There was nothing more painful for a White man than to see the image of a Negro mixed in with the image of the woman he was married to. In front of me at a three-foot distance was the barrel of the revolver that had killed my mother. This man's eyes were filled with nothing but lust, filth, and vile for me, and I would surely die before I would let his hands ever touch me.

"You will have to kill me, sir," I stated, backing toward the farthest edge of the boulders.

"I just might have to, since it seems like you don't have any place else to go," he said. While I thought that maybe Royce would contemplate his next move as opposed to acting impulsively, I quickly found out I was wrong.

10

McKinley

"Love not when all is forsaken."

One hundred lashes. That was anybody's punishment for trying to run away from the Wellsworth Plantation. Blood finally began to drip from Blue's back as his body maintained its composure in the hogshead I kept out in the shed. He was a big, fine nigger, probably one of the biggest in Virginia, standing well over six feet tall. With his body almost folded up inside of the hoops, I tried to cut into his hide like a sickle wrapping my whip around every curve in his body. By lash forty, he was still holdin' his head in the air. The muscles that were evenly spread across his back welcomed every strike, and for a minute at first, I ain't think the nigger had no blood running through him because he just would not bleed. So I swung harder.

"You a uppity nigger, ain't you boy?"

Blue ain't say nothing, and as I watched his glistening ebony skin swell from the impressions made from my mule skinner, I swung even harder the next time, eventually cracking the surface of his welts.

"Did you hear me, nigger?"

He still ain't answer. Tiny specks of nigger blood sprayed across my forehead when I popped the blood-soaked strip against his skin...again.

Lash seventy. Lunging backwards with the force of the wind and the strength of ten bulls behind the whip, I struck Blue, watching the veins in his neck stiffen with every blow. I ain't care about all his folks standing around carrying on like he was about to die. Don't no nigger try to run from McKinley Wellsworth's place and live to tell about it. His little daughter, Katie, clutched her mammy's apron with one arm and covered her eyes with the other. With every thrash, Blue's body twitched.

"Still ain't gone answer me, boy, huh?"

Tch-tch-tch-tch-tch. Lashes seventy-one, seventy-two, seventy-three, seventy-four, and seventy-five.

"Plez, an'sr Marse, Pa. Plez," Katie whined.

I ain't care nothing about what that gal said to him. Answering me or not, Blue had it coming to him. See, the other week I took Blue, Cal, and Webster with me to Hampton to pick up some supplies. That kind of trip usually took about a day or two; depending on how many stops you made. Cal drove the wagon there, and Blue and Webster were there to help load everything up. On the way back, it started raining pretty bad and then one of the wheels fell off the wagon when we hit what looked like a crater in the road. The wheel like-d split in half, and lucky for me, I always carried a hammer and some nails in the back of the wagon.

All through the rain, them niggers worked to get that wheel fixed. I ain't never had no troubles out of none of them so I ain't see no harm in me taking a little nap until they finished. Morning come, and I looked around and seen them laying around like cattle next to this big oak tree. I walked over and seen Cal and Webster but no Blue.

"Whar, Blue?" I asked. Neither Cal nor Webster said a word.

They rose to they feet, and no sooner than they stood up straight I hauled off and hit Cal 'cause he was the weakest of the two. "You hear me, boy?"

"Ya suh," he mumbled. "I ain't seed Blue since we laid down, suh. He were ri' thar when we wents t'sleep."

You know niggers ain't too quick to turn on they own sometimes; especially if the one that done run off done promised to come for them. It was useless trying to get anything out of Cal, and knowing Webster, he really ain't know nothing neither. The only thing I said to them was, "You better pray to the good Lord that the slave catchers get him and kill him before I do." They stood there like two idiots until I told them to load up the wagon.

That next Sunday while all us White folks was sitting in church, we heard some commotion approaching, and me and some of the other men got up to see what all the ruckus was about. Dogs was barking so loud it seemed they was right up at the front door of the church. Pastor Dukes stopped preaching and went over to the winder to see what was going on. Coming up the road was Gus Meyer, the nigger slave catcher from the North. He made a good amount of money catching niggers and taking them back to their masters. Heard that one time he even took one of his own relatives back to the plantation. It weren't no secret, though, that he was working with some White man up in Maryland. He paid him ten dollars for every slave he collected on. Behind his horse, he was pulling some fifteen-twenty niggers, and right there with them was Blue. Spending money on runaway niggers was a waste to me, but, here I was in front of everybody and I knew I was going to have to pay to get this piece of shit back. "McKinley Wellsworth," Gus announced.

"Boy, you better get yourself right. You in Virginia now." I had to knock him off that high horse he rode in here on.

Gus went to pulling in his lip, and he knew he could not get a lick done without doing what was right. "Mister McKinley Wellsworth, sir, one of these here niggers say he belong to you."

My first mind was to say nothing because any slaves that went unclaimed was taken to the auction. But it meant more to me to make an example out of Blue. "Yeah, that one right thar belong to me. How much?" Blue's clothes was damn near torn to shreds, and his foot looked like the one of the dogs had done got after him.

"Two-hundred, suh."

"What? Boy, I give you fifty dollars for that darkie and not a penny more."

Gus got down off his horse and took his hat off. "Suh, I kindly respect your offer, but two-hundred is what I charge to bring him back to you."

Looking around at the folks who was watching as to whether or not I was gone have the upper hand, I walked over to Gus and looked him square in the eyes. "Well, for that, you can care him on back to where you found him. He ain't worth that kind of money with a bad leg no how." I glanced over at Blue with his heading hanging at the ground, and the more I thought about it, I said, "Forty is all I gives you for him." I pulled out some folded bills from my pocket and tossed the money at his feet.

Gus, bellowing at my gesture, bent over to pick up the money. Just as he reached for it, I stepped on his hand and did my best to crush every bone in his hand. "From now on, if a runaway nigger tell you he belong to me, do him a favor and go head on and kill him."

❖❖❖

T-ch. Lash ninety-nine. Blue's body looked like it ain't have no more life in it. His head was buckled down between two logs, his mangled body no longer stiff. I'd broke away most of the wood in the hogshead so he could crawl through the hoops and then I could tie his body to the cinder blocks supporting it. I know that nigger wished he never ran away. My blood was boiling 'cause Blue still ain't never answer me.

Resting the mule skinner underneath my arm, I stepped back for a minute to light the embers in my pipe and take a few puffs to relax my nerves. I walked toward the narrow opening to the shed and leaned up against the wall to ponder my next move. Despite the fact Blue was naked, the bystanders was itching to help him. They was doing they best to not eyeball me 'cause they wanted to go over and see about him.

"Gone over thar," I said to them but ain't nobody move. "You hear what I say? Gone on. Get." Slowly, one by one, they started strolling over to Blue; trying to kiss on him and cut him loose. "Naw, naw, now. Don't you be trying to set him free. He still got one more lash to get." He was not dead. I could hear his moans and grunts when they was touching on him.

I try real hard to never let a nigger think I give a damn about him, his ways or his family, but that little one, Katie, I watches her. I know she likely Edward's, like most of the children on the plantation is, but her presence is a bit different to me. She got tight, curly hair like her mammy with skin just a little lighter than Blue's, but her eyes is green like my family's. Any wench I done ever had, I sold her on way from here after a while. Katie, though, looked plenty enough like me for me to wonder if I let one slip past. I'd been with so many of my slaves it was hard trying to keep up with all of them. Standing there taking more draws from my pipe, I watched Katie rub Blue's head and wipe it with the hem of her dress. She rested her head against his and held it there. I turned my back when Katie started to cry. "Ples, Papa. It gone be fine. Be jes fine. We gone git you up from here an'take good care uh you," she whimpered.

I'd had enough. "Gone, gal," I demanded. "Get on way so I can finish this." Katie ran back over to her mammy, weeping out of control. I pulled the mule skinner from my armpit and stood just above Blue's head. I leaned over in his ear and said, "Boy, you ain't answer me from before. Is you a uppity nigger?"

If he had any sense, he might of spoke right up. I ain't never know a nigger to have good sense, and Blue ain't let me down. I dropped my whip and exchanged it for the revolver in my holster. Without even looking at him and aiming where I heard life, I unloaded one round into Blue's head, splattering flesh and brains across my boots and onto the hay on the ground below. Then I put my embers out in the open flesh across his back and went on about my business.

❋❋❋

The pink-eyed white devil is what the folks around these parts call me. When the Lord gave out good looks, He plain ol' skipped right over me and gave them to my brother, Edward. He was a decent sized man with green eyes and thick, brown hair. The girls used to run up to him and throw kisses on him without him even asking for them. Instead of any type of compassion, they threw rocks and sticks at me. I wore a larger than normal hat to cover my eyes from the sunlight. My skin and hair was whiter than snow, and when the sun got to it, it burned something awful. It cracked and peeled 'til it looked like my skin come clear off. My mother got salve from the doctor to keep my skin from getting infected, and sometimes that ain't even work for me. Finally, she started sending me to school with every inch of my body covered. One day my brother Edward and my cousin, Henry, let the other children lock me out of the schoolhouse after recess while the weather was blazing hot. I knocked on the door as hard as I could, but no one ever came to let me in. I ran to all the windows, slamming my hands against the glass until they ran red with blood. I could see everything right in front of me but nothing far away. Since most of my life I had been treated like I weren't there—almost invisible—my teacher, Miss MacIntosh, who was slightly hard of hearing, ain't notice right off I weren't in the room. I could hear her going on with the lesson while the others was laughing at me.

"Class, tell me, please, what is so humorous that I can't keep your attention this afternoon." The laughter stopped. "Oh, so now, you have not a thing to say?" Still silence. "Well, let's keep it silent so we might proceed with our lesson."

It was amazing to me, she couldn't hear my screams or my pounding on the doors and windows. After a while, I got tired and sat down on the steps outside. Going home without my brother would've only cause me more problems 'cause my daddy told Edward to look after me. Edward, in front of the family, did look after me, but it was when he was around his friends and Henry that his mean streak came out. So many times he told me he wished I was dead and said I'd never be welcomed in heaven 'cause God ain't make people like me.

Only the devil could make something so horribly ugly. When-ever we sat in church, I sat between my parents, at first, because I thought they loved me and wanted to protect me. I later found out it was because the pastor had told them no one else wanted to sit by, what many had begun to call me, the pink-eyed white devil.

After hours of waiting on the steps, I finally heard the door open and looked up to see Mavis Crump standing over me. "Come on in. Miss MacIntosh told me to come out here and get you."

Cooked like pigskin, I walked in and took my seat. The students were doing a writing lesson, and Miss MacIntosh was sitting at her desk and never looked up at me. Edward and Henry both took glances of me but never gave me the attention I needed at the time. Tears that had fell were dried on my face, and my hands trembled from intense pain. My brother and cousin snickered at me as I struggled to write. I felt the skin over my fingers split, and I watched my blood seep through the openings.

Mavis, who by now had got tired of Edward and Henry, pulled a tattered cloth from his pocket and handed it to me. I was grateful for Mavis's kindness because, quite frankly, I thought no one gave a damn about McKinley Wellsworth. All the way home that afternoon, rocks and sticks was still throwed at me. Once my mother saw the burns about my body, she convinced my daddy to keep me home from school and spend time helping him with tending to the plantation. "You're not a handsome man by any account, McKinley, and you never will be," she said. I had believed that at least your mother would make you feel special when no one else could, but that night her words brought my heartbeat to a halt. Later at supper, I listened as Edward and my daddy talked about the world like I weren't even in it. I couldn't eat 'cause my stomach was in knots. I ain't trust my brother as far as I could see him. He had done stood by and let everybody make fun of me, and, when he could, he did the same.

After a spell, my mother got up from the table and retired to her room. While I was helping Beckett clear the dishes, my spirit wept 'cause there was no passion in my family, and if there was, they never showed it to me. When I reached for my daddy's plate, he grabbed my wrist and cackled with the smell of the devil's juice on his breath. "You might as well get used to the cruelness of the world, son, and get used to cleaning up after yourself 'cause unlessen you plan to have a bunch of niggers working your land, you ain't gone never get a wife."

II

I called her Lizzie because Lisbeth seemed to be so formal-like to me. I met her early in the evening on the same day I'd finished my business with Blue. She was visiting with her mother, Miss Lucy, down near Carter's Grove, and I'd come down there for a meeting with Mavis, who lived a little ways from Miss Lucy's place. Mavis, a lawyer and politician, and I had been hunting together since we were lads and now devoted much our time doing what we could to promote and protect the sanctity of slavery. Mavis was back and forth to Richmond in his dealings with the legislature, and in between them times, we visited with Miss Lucy to keep her company in her old age. She lived alone and was always talking about the life she used to have down in Georgia. Honestly, for a good while, we ain't never believe her.

"I used to have my own slaves and land before I come to Williamsburg," she was always saying to us. "That old hussie Jake had living there don't know nothing about running no plantation. One day I'm going get my house back and everything in it. You wait and see." The strangest thing about it was she didn't have a lick of proof of the life she once had. "When my husband died, he left me with money and slaves. I got a beautiful daughter, too," she bragged. "I'm waiting on Lisbeth to get here so she can help me get it." Miss Lucy, in her early seventies, was in and out her right mind most of the time, and Mavis and me would simply sit in the rocking chairs on her front porch and just listen.

As I walked up the gravel path to Miss Lucy's porch, I took time to study my boots to make sure there wasn't any mud or dirt on them so as to not track any onto the landing. What looked a lump of dried mud turned out to be a piece of brain from Blue. Staring at the imperfection resting atop my boot, I never regretted how it got there. For me it was a symbol of my loyalty to the South and my determination to keep the institution of slavery alive in Virginia. It served as warning to the next nigger that thought about running away. The front door was open, and I peeped through the screen and only saw Hannah standing in the parlor. Pressing my face up against the mesh, I called out, "Gal, whar's Miss Lucy?"

Hannah ain't answer me right back. Instead, she wiped her hands on her apron and hurried in the other direction.

"Gal, don't make me come in there after you. Whar's..." Next thing I know I heard footsteps rushing toward me.

My eyesight had worsened over the years, and all I could make out was fuzz at first. Squinting my eyes, I managed to focus on the image of a woman with her arm stretched out hurrying toward the door. *Crack!* Then everything went black.

❂❂❂

"McKinley?" someone whispered. It was Mavis. "You all right?" The sky was spinning as I tried to lift my head from the ground.

"My Lord, what on earth happened?" My head was stinging like somebody had done slapped me with a brick.

Looking down at me, Mavis repeatedly slapped his knee as he chuckled. "The lady doesn't take too well to peeping toms."

I rose to my feet, clutching my forehead with one hand and dusting my britches off and picking up my hat with the other. "What lady? Miss Lucy ain't…"

At that moment, a breath of fresh air fell upon me as one of God's angels emerged from the house with a damp rag stretched over cubes of ice. "Evening, Mr. Wellsworth. I'm Lisbeth… Lucy's daughter."

With amber eyes and soft, curly reddish-brown hair, she was nothing but beautiful to me. She hadn't been long left her husband for whatever reason. That wasn't my business, to know where she had come from. My only concern was to know what I could do to make the rest of Lizzie's life better than what it had already been.

"Well, the pleasure's all mine. How'd you do?" I asked, bowing before her.

"Better than you, I suppose. Here, put this ice on your head to keep the swelling down. My mother's told me all about you, Mr. Wellsworth. She speaks real high of you and Mr. Crump. Please take a seat," she offered.

"Much obliged, ma'am." I staggered to the empty seat next to her, and as Hannah came through the door to bring us all some lemonade, I plopped my boot against the wooden railing that extended from one side of the porch to the other, so she could see what was left of Blue. He used to come around and do some carpentry for Miss Lucy before I'd been told he was being a little too fresh with Hannah. He wasn't getting his work done, and whatever work that he did do was done poorly. She'd overheard me telling Mavis and Miss Lucy that I'd never let him see the light of day if he was ever caught.

"My mother tells me you finally got that nigger who run off from you."

Placing the ice pack on my head, I answered, "Yeah, I got him, and he's all over and done with now. It's nothing a pretty lady like you needs to be worrying about." The sun was disappearing over the trees, making it easier for me to see. I simply ain't want to take my eyes off this woman.

Lizzie hesitated slightly before putting her soft fingertips against the spot where the door had slapped me. "Got licked pretty good," she joked, seeing the rising knot. "You need to make sure you keep that ice on it for as long as you can."

Besides my mother and Miss Lucy, ain't no woman ever expressed an interest in me, so I weren't used to the attention. For a good while, she sat there on that porch talking to me and Mavis like we was all ol' friends. Every word she spoke to me set upon my heart and found a way to make an impression on my mind. I wondered if she saw my imperfections and felt pity for me and kept talking to me only out of kindness. It even crossed my mind that maybe she was trying to get Mavis's attention, but all the while she kept up her conversation with me. Then when Mavis left to head on home, she paused only for a minute to say good-bye and continued talking to me. Befo' I knew it, night started creeping in. The stinging in my head had long stopped, and I'd been scared to tell her that, thinking she might cut our visit short.

"Well, ma'am, I have to get on back my way befo' my darkies begin to think that they run the place."

While she had been rocking back and forth in her chair, seems like the entire time we'd been talking, Lizzie abruptly stopped and asked, "Why, I'm sure things are all right. If it's supper you're worried about, then I can have Hannah rustle you up something."

Only the good Lord knew how bad I wanted to sit with her—all night if I could, but I had to get on home. "I'm sorry, ma'am, but I have to go." I rose from my chair and grabbed my hat that was hanging on the back of my chair. "But, ma'am, if you don't mind, I would like to call on you tomorrow."

Charmed by my request, Lizzie answered, "Well, I would like that very much, McKinley Wellsworth."

❁❁❁

Unlike most children of my time, I worked on the plantation long side the slaves slopping the hogs, filling the troughs, and cleaning the stables. My family's wealth was in tobacco, and, before Daddy died, he spoke with Mavis about making sure Edward was in control of everything. I ain't never fool myself into thinking anything different would've happened. Daddy had done pretty good for himself and the family name by bartering our tobacco with merchants and shopkeepers for items such as clothing, furniture, and wine. On occasion he traded it for slaves; especially if it was getting close to harvest time. A few years before his death, Daddy started shipping the tobacco to England to be sold and soon became one of the wealthiest men in Virginia.

As a boy we lived in a two-story home with two rooms downstairs that included a large bedroom where my parents slept.

Edward and I slept in a room upstairs where we had to keep dark drapes up to the windows or keep the shutters closed. Edward ain't like it much, so he often crept downstairs and got in bed with my parents. As the quality of life began to improve for us, Daddy wanted a bigger home for us, so construction was begun on a home to be located next door to the old one. Months before it was complete, my mother gave birth to a little girl, Beth Marie, but both she and both my mother took sick and died a few days after she was born. I was never sure about how all of that affected Daddy because he never showed feelings about anything. He did, however, stop sleeping in our old house the day she died and made us move into the new house before it was finished. There was an ice house, dairy house, smoke house, cook house, and burial grounds, which is where he buried my sister and mother.

While we ain't have very many slaves in the beginning, the number increased as the demand for our tobacco crops increased. Included on the grounds of our Georgian mansion was an extensive servants' quarters site that could house over two hundred slaves. Each servant had a designated chore to be completed around the plantation. We were generally good to our slaves, but, whenever there was word of uprisings on other plantations, we tightened up on them by watching every move they made and performing daily head counts. Running away was painted as a picture of the ultimate betrayal and was dealt with by a simple bullet to the head to stop the thinking process altogether. Daddy, who was leery of outsiders, charged Edward with being the overseer. Needless to say, I ended up being the one doing all the work but never got any credit for it. Edward made sure he was able to have his way with the females, and, as punishment for those who were unwilling, he made them sleep with me. It was like being forced to sleep with the devil, as he used to say.

Quite naturally, I was jealous of Edward. He was the one that got to go into town with Daddy, making the rounds at all the businesses. "This is my son, Edward. I want you all to get to know him because one day my stay on this earth will be done, and he will be the one in charge," he'd always say.

"You must be proud, Easton. He's a fine boy," he'd get in return as they looked into the back of the wagon at me as I sat there covered in my floppy hat. I never thought any of it was fair, but, like I told you, the two of them was good for carrying on in the world like I was never in it.

Not long after the dust settled on Daddy's grave, Edward put me out of the main house, which was finally finished in 1804, and sent me to the stay in our old home. Dwarfed by the grandeur of the estate, the home offered the bare necessities and actually stripped me of the life of which I become accustomed. Nearly every room had two windows with no draperies or shutters so I ain't have no way to protect myself from the sunlight. The only space in the house with no sunlight was a closet on the lower level that wasn't even big enough for me to slide a bed into. Every night I retired to a pile of straw and a blanket while my brother slept on fine linens and commandeered all the servants worthy to be in the house to cater to all his wants and needs. After church on Sundays, Edward used the dinner on the grounds as a chance for him to charm the ladies— both unmarried and married. He knew the dowries of all the unmarried women, for many of their fathers did some type of business with him. And then, those married women with husbands who desired to do business with Edward disclosed their inheritances to him in hopes of securing a working relationship with my brother. I recall one particular young lady with curly blonde hair and gray eyes by the name of Mary Alice Courtland, who was married to Ignatius Courtland, II. Born of British aristocracy, Mary Alice was the wealthiest woman in the region but had married a man known for accumulating large amounts of gambling debts. Ignatius did any and everything to protect himself from losing his fortune. To settle a debt, he approached Edward after church one Sunday about borrowing a large sum of money, without involving his wife in the matter. Dressed in a grey short jacket and long waistcoat with a matching grey top hat encircled with a dark grey band, Ignatius walked over to where Edward and I were standing. "Good day, Edward," Ignatius greeted.

"Ignatius," Edward responded cordially but curt. My brother was not the least bit of fond of Ignatius because of his unstable business dealings, which sometimes affected how their mutual business associates treated him in their financial transactions. Sunday after Sunday, Edward followed Mary Alice's every move, and every now and again I would catch her doing the same.

"Might I have a minute with you?" Ignatius requested.

With his hands in the pockets of his breeches, Edward replied, "You may."

Glancing over at me, Ignatius asked, "Alone?"

"My brother is a part of me, and whatever business you have with me, you have with him." That, I knew, was malarkey.

Hesitantly, he continued, "Very well, then. I'm sure you are aware of my business ventures and how, as proprietors, we all have to make sacrifices to ensure the success of those ventures."

"I'm quite well aware of such things, Ignatius, but it doesn't take a smart man to know you've always been careless in your ventures, which is why you are having this conversation with me."

Ignatius, a man of keen, dark features reflecting his Indian heritage, began to loosen the high collar around his neck and wiped his brow with a handkerchief he pulled from his pocket. "Right then, well, I was wondering if you would consider loaning this gentleman…"

"You surely must be joking, good sir. You haven't a dime to your name that isn't already promised to here or thither. Be serious. Why would I loan you a penny, when you have not the means to repay it?"

Muddled by the suggestion, Ignatius spoke, "How dare you pretend to be God and judge me such as you have?"

Edward didn't have many friends for a number of reasons; the main one was his arrogance. "Perhaps you should be speaking to Him, then, about your problems and not to me, or is it that you feel you would owe Him less if you ask Him?"

"What?"

Watching Mary Alice as the coachman helped her into the carriage, Edward, with a glazed stare, offered, "I will loan you the money you desire, but your repayment will be far more than the mere pennies you request."

"That's understandable. I'm prepared to pay interest to you; if that's what you mean."

"No, that is not what I mean, Ignatius. You will repay me with your wife. You will allow her to come to me and make me a happy man whenever I ask."

"Are you mad, Edward Wellsworth?" Ignatius, while a seemingly happily married man, was desperate. "I will have to give some thought to this, but it is highly unlikely it will happen."

It was obvious he was embarrassed by Edward's proposal and even more so that I had heard it.

"Then our business here is done."

My brother turned and instructed me to go and fetch our horses. As I began to walk away, I looked over my shoulder to see what Edward's next move was to be. To my surprise it was nothing. Ignatius hurried to the waiting carriage and, after five minutes or so of sitting, it pulled off. Later that night, as I returned to my house to retire for the evening, I was greeted by the same carriage and in it was Mary Alice. The late night meetings of Mary Alice and Edward continued for several months until it became quite apparent that the two had produced a blond, curly-haired, green-eyed heir to both fortunes named Ignatius Courtland, III; and there wasn't a thing Ignatius Courtland, II, could do about it. Mary Alice, however, made sure her son was knowledgeable of his parentage, so there was one more person between me and the family business.

As Edward approached his mid-forties, he started having trouble remembering the simplest of things, and, while his mistreatment of me had not changed much, he began to rely on me for help with recalling his dealings. Since I had not much experience in his affairs, I, in turn, called upon Mavis who had been schooled far more than me. He had spent several years in England learning the ways of the Brits and even traveled to other countries such as China and Japan. It was he who bought me a pair of blue-green tinted glasses to help protect my eyes from the sun. Having studied the laws of many lands, Mavis was sharp and disgusted when he returned to Williamsburg and learned of the injustices done to me by Edward. "Mavis, I'd do anything in this world for my brother."

"Shoot, why? He obviously doesn't give a damn about you."

"He's my blood, and it's simply the right thing to do."

Mavis got up from his chair and walked over to a box sitting on his mahogany desk. He reached into his pocket, pulled out a ring of keys, and began peeling through them until he got to the smallest one. Sticking it in the keyhole, he smirked. "Sometimes it takes the smallest thing to open you up to the biggest surprises. Come over here for a minute. I want to show you something."

As a lawyer, he always used more words than needed to get his message across. When he opened the box, I approached the desk and saw several stacks of folded papers on top. Mavis lifted them all, placing the stacks on the desk next to the box. The only thing left in there was an envelope with my family's name written on the outside of it. Mavis gestured for me to take a seat in an adjacent chair and then began opening the envelope.

"You know, I don't believe in holding grudges, McKinley, nor do I believe in treating people unfairly. However, from the day I opened those doors to the classroom and saw you sitting there in utter misery to now, I have held a special place for you in my heart. Day after day, I watched you work that land of your father's with not even the simplest of gratitude. Then the day he came to me and asked me to create this document giving total control of his estate to Edward in the event of his death, it sickened me to see how a father chose one son over the other. There was not one mention of you during the whole discussion, but I continued to do what he *thought* I was doing."

"I'm having a bit of trouble understanding what you're talking about."

"The entire time your daddy was telling me about all this tremendous fortune he had and the things he had put in place to make your brother a very rich man, I was writing down everything. He became so carried away with himself that he signed his will without reading over it properly and missed the fact that I'd put your name down as the sole beneficiary, instead of Edward's."

"And you did not fix it?"

"No, I didn't. I had seen you work your fingers to the bone around that place and had I changed it, you would've never gotten your due. So, what I'm saying, my friend, is that everything Edward has barely worked to keep is really yours, and it is good things have remained in such great condition."

"But what about his son?"

"What about him?"

"Does he not have a claim to any of this?"

"Only if you choose for him to."

Dumbfounded by the whole matter, I snatched the document from Mavis so I could read it for myself. My vision had worsened over the years and seemed to completely disappear when I tried to make out words. I fumbled through my coat pocket for my glasses to help me make out the words that would change my life. "This will kill him, Mavis."

"I'm sure it will, but it should only be our secret for a while," he said, taking the document from me and placing it back in the envelope.

"Why is that?"

"Look," Mavis said, putting the envelope back in the box. "You, yourself told me Edward's becoming forgetful."

"Yes, Mavis, he is, but he still has most of his wits about him."

"The time will come when all of this will matter. Please trust me, McKinley. In the meantime, carry on as usual. It won't last much longer."

❁❁❁

Miss Lucy moved to Williamsburg, seems like around 1810, by way of the Carolinas, and settled into a modest house not too far from Denbigh. Mavis and I met her in Williamsburg one day as she strolled along in front of what used to be the Capitol on Duke of Gloucester Street. Asking us for directions to an acquaintance's house, Miss Lucy made a lot of extra small talk with us, and the next thing we knew, she'd invited us to her house for supper. Every so often I caught her staring, but that didn't go on for long. "Pardon me for staring so, but I've never seen the likes of you where I come from."

"And where is it you come from, ma'am?" I smiled. I'd not had much contact with women before I met Miss Lucy. While I believed my mother loved me, she was truly afraid of what society held for me, not being able to understand or accept my abnormalities. Edward and Henry had made life miserable for me, emotionally, by convincing me of the fact that no woman would ever want me and that the only way I could have natural fulfillment was to take it from the slaves.

In front of the family, they protected me and appeared to show me love, but, when no one else was around, things changed. Many of the girls I knew from school had laughed at me, and those who didn't find any humor in my existence adopted fear. I'd tried to give them flowers and candies, but they were often thrown to the ground and stepped on as the young ladies walked away. The servants feared me as they did every other White man, but, for me, it was different. Granted, I was a monster in their eyes but even monsters take on the form of the devil sometimes, and everybody's afraid of him.

"I'm from all over, I guess, but if I had to claim somewhere, it'd be Augusta down in Georgia. I had a family, land, slaves, and all down there, but my husband asked to me leave so he could house his whore. I left there and spent a little time in Charleston and made my way to Greensboro." She kept her eyes on me the entire time she spoke, and I surmised it was because of mere curiosity.

Walking over to me with a boldness not seen in many women around our parts, Miss Lucy demanded, "Take them glasses off, sir, so I can see your eyes. I have to see a person's eyes when I talk to them. That's the way I begin to trust somebody." Bewildered by her request, Mavis looked to me as if to suggest I oblige Miss Lucy and reveal my eyes. With the sun shining brilliantly upon my countenance, I removed my glasses, squinting my eyes and shielding them from the sun's rays.

Miss Lucy peered into my colorless pupils and then ordered me to put them back on. "Sorry about that, mister, mister…"

"It's McKinley Wellsworth, ma'am, and this is my good friend, Mavis Crump."

"Well, it's been a pleasure meeting both of you. I must get on my way, but you should come by my house some time and sit a spell."

Glancing at Mavis for his reaction, I approved for the both of us. "We shall perhaps do that one day soon."

❂❂❂

After I'd gotten better acquainted with her over the years, I learned Miss Lucy was a gentle woman with genuine tendencies, and she was one of the few people I could trust. Against Mavis's wishes, I shared with her the fortune I was entitled to when the time was right. Many times she'd encountered Edward at the house and was the first outsider to recognize he was losing his mind. "You should claim what's yours, McKinley, because, believe me, that brother of yours is not going to ever give it to you."

"Mavis told me I should wait. It's best for everybody."

"What the hell does Mavis know? He ain't had to go through what you have. Ever noticed how his beady, little eyes shift back and forth?"

Miss Lucy had a tendency to overreact by over-assessing people and their actions. It was exceptionally hard, getting her to trust anyone.

"Miss Lucy, I've known Mavis most of my life, and he has never misguided me."

"Horse shit. He's a lawyer, McKinley. That's all he knows how to do."

❂❂❂

For months after that discussion, I found myself questioning Miss Lucy's reasoning for thinking Mavis wasn't the friend he'd proven himself to be. Life went on as usual, but now under a guise of suspicion about who I could trust.

12

The spring of 1836 turned to summer and summer to fall, and, by the time the winter was getting ready to come, Miss Lucy left us for a journey with Jesus. She died at home surrounded by Lizzie, Edward, Mavis, Pastor Dukes, myself and Hannah. As Pastor prayed over her corpse, Hannah began drawing the blinds and closing the shutters. She then walked around the rest of us and over to Miss Lucy's chifforobe where she pulled out several pieces of black crepe from a drawer. Taking them with her, she headed to the front door and opened it. There she tied one piece of the fabric to the doorknocker and another piece to the top of the archway above the outside of the entry door.

I followed Hannah as best I could with my eyes as she went from space to space, covering next the mantle and then picture frames. Making her way back to the bedroom, Hannah stretched another piece of the crinkly black fabric over the dresser mirror as she looked away from her reflection. Finally, in one swift effort, she turned the cheval mirror to the wall—avoiding her own image. Puzzled by the gestures, I slowly walked over to the dresser to perhaps gain a better understanding of this ritual. The one thing, though, that I realized was that I was about to see myself, for I had not done so since I was a young boy. I had seen strands of my hair up on my jackets and in my comb, but was able to determine I'd never know if and when my hair turned gray. As I got closer to the mirror, I prepared myself by closing eyes and extended my arms to guide me to the edge of the dresser. Grasping the corners, I stood ready to face myself.

"No, suh, Marse," Hannah's voice rang out. "You mustn't do that." Her frantic call disturbed the solemn mood of the room and startled me because she grabbed me from behind. "Suh, if-n you looks in te dat mirrah, you shall be da next te die for sho'."

Without err, I turned and slapped Hannah across the mouth, knocking her to the floor. "Gal, don't you ever put your filthy nigger hands on me again," I warned quietly. "You understand me?"

"Yessuh, Marse," she whimpered, scooting backwards across the floor. She scrambled to her feet and rushed to another room in the house. Not heeding Hannah's warning, my desire to see my reflection had not gone away. More hurriedly than before, I turned back to the mirror and swept the fabric to the side. Gazing into the mirror, I indeed saw a monster. My hair had grown past my shoulders, and my bleached skin was free of the wrinkles that plagued my brother. I had seen more than forty years on earth and wondered if I'd ever find a love to settle down with. Running my fingers across my pale pink lips, I imagined what they would feel like pressed against another's. How could someone have love for a man such as me? And children? There was no way anyone would want a child who could possibly look like a freak of nature. Disgusted with what I was forced to have lived with all of my life, I returned the fabric to its first position and moved away from the dresser. Hannah's words haunted me. Would I be the next to die before experiencing true love?

❀❀❀

Miss Lucy's body was driven by wagon to the burial ground on my plantation, which sat on a hill overlooking Carter's Grove. When I first asked Edward about the circumstances upon which I was making my request, he immediately said no. He hadn't been fond of Miss Lucy nor Lizzie, for he considered them to be misplaced poor white trash preying on wealthy men. He knew I had great admiration for both women, but it still didn't matter to him.

I said, "Edward, if your presumption about them is that they're looking for a rich husband, then shouldn't they be looking to befriend you?"

My rhetoric didn't impress him. "The answer is no, McKinley. I haven't planted the seeds of fortune upon my plantation to have it tainted by the rotting corpses of Southern belle misfits. Those women have no more refinement in them than any of the niggers we have running around here."

Edward's memory was always worst at night, and there was no reasonable explanation as to why. A few times he stumbled into my house and asked what I had done with all the furniture. Not taking his actions seriously, I scoffed, "I gave it all away, Edward. Don't you remember?"

I was expecting him to perhaps frown a little, or maybe even yell at me. Instead, he stood there in the doorway, scratching his head and simply said, "Okay." Then he turned and walked out the door.

Another time he burst into the house, sat down at the table

and asked for a cup of hot tea. Katie, who I'd gotten to work around the house for me, prepared the tea for him and also gave him a peach tea biscuit to go with it. Several minutes passed, and within that time, Edward had devoured a half dozen biscuits and three cups of tea. I got the feeling he was waiting on something or someone. Taking the sleeve of his jacket and wiping his mouth, he asked, "Did you see the dress I got for Beth Marie? I'm waiting for her to come downstairs so I can see her in it before we go to church."

At that moment, I knew something was wrong. So, like the many times he had used me to get his way or mistreated me, it was my time to do the same. "Well, she's coming soon, Edward. She wants to wear her new dress to Miss Lucy's funeral. Would that be okay with you?"

He didn't answer me right away. Matter of fact, he seemed to be drifting off to sleep. "Miss Lucy?" he asked, yawning.

"Yes, Miss Lucy. Remember, you said we could bury her next to our mother and father up at the cemetery?"

"Right, right, I sure did. Well, we can all go and pay our respects to the family. I'll get on back up to the house and have something cooked up for them." And just as he had several times before, Edward turned and disappeared into the darkness.

❂❂❂

Watching Lizzie over the next several weeks was difficult for me. She was distant from me and everyone else around her. After the funeral, she remained in Williamsburg and got a room at the inn on Duke of Gloucester Street. I would ride by there around two in the afternoon every day when I knew she'd be sitting outside about to have tea. Still dressed in mourning attire, she would receive me and sometimes Mavis, when he wasn't visiting with his friend, Nathaniel Tucker, over at the College of William and Mary. The two of them, along with two other gentlemen, were working toward creating the ground-work for a law school. Quite frankly, I thought it to be a waste of time, but Mavis saw it more as an opportunity for him to grow. It all paid off for him because he's the man you want fighting for you whenever those nigger agitators come around here. Any-how, I wondered if Lizzie knew I was coming by just to lay eyes on her. I was too bashful to actually go up to her in front of everyone, and I didn't want everyone's eyes on her, thinking real mean of her because she was speaking to the likes of me.

Several times before, I had ridden past the blacksmith's shop, wanting to stop in and get new shoes for my horse, but neglected to stop. There were always too many people coming in and out of there, and, at all costs, I wanted to avoid humiliation. On this date, however, there were no other customers, so I figured it a good time to stop in. As I dismounted my horse, a young girl, who had to be no more than about six or seven, approached me with a folded piece of paper and a mint in her hand. "For this piece of candy I have here, the lady in black asked me to give this letter to you," she said innocently as her hands, dressed in tightly-fitted white gloves, trembled with fear.

Looking from east to west, I did not see a woman in black, but I thanked the child who was all but too eager to leave my sight. I unfolded the note laced with the scent of roses and peered through my glasses as best I could to make out the words. I had not yet come to the realization that my ability to see words and some images was vanishing. "Excuse me, sir, could you...?" I asked a gentleman as he rushed past me. The next person I attempted to ask did the same as did the next and the next. Soon, having grown tired of the rejection, I mounted my horse and headed home.

As my horse trotted toward the front door of the mansion, I saw Katie sweeping the walk in front of my house. "Gal, where is Master Edward?"

Pushing the broom meticulously across the bricks buried in the ground, she replied, "He in da hows, Marse. Bin dare all day."

I was so anxious to have someone read what Lizzie had written that I jumped off my horse and didn't bother tying the reins to the stake. I boyishly skipped into the house and found Edward sitting in the parlor. He was reading the paper while the servants cleaned around him.

"Edward?" I asked, trying to catch my breath.

Never looking up at me, he answered sternly, "What is it, McKinley?"

I'd grown used to his lack of compassion for me, but my heart, as it quivered with glee, needed some resolve to the matter quickly. Pulling the piece of paper from the inside of my coat pocket, I handed it to him and took a seat on the Queen Anne settee which complemented the Queen Anne chairs he'd had imported from England.

"I got this note from Lizzie, and I am having trouble reading it. My eyes are not what they used to be."

Placing his spectacles over his nose, Edward reared back in his chair and perused the note. Seemingly at every other word, he peered over the top of the paper to look at me. "I see," he commented. "For the life of me, I can't understand why you insist on having dealings with her, but it seems here that you have a bit of an admirer."

Full of happiness, I requested, "Please read it for me, Edward."
Edward began:

"'*McKinley, love from afar is harder felt than love that is near. I
see you peeping in and around corners. Might you come to me and
express your fancy? God has taken my mother from me, but He has
blessed with me another angel to watch over me.*

Very truly yours, Lizzie.'"

Unable to find words, my eyes uttered them for me as tears
formed a downward path on my cheeks. I reached for the paper
but was overcome by extreme joy. "I…"

"Don't try to speak, brother. It's easy to see you are trounced
with unspeakable bliss. I shall keep the letter here with me to
protect it. Any time you want me to read it to you, I will."

My heart was filled with amorous desires too vivid to convey
upon my brother, so I rushed home and began to display my
affections in words.

"*Dearest, Lizzie:*

*At first sight, my eyes rested upon a beast not known to man—only
to angels. Your magnificent splendor radiated my heart as I tried to
keep time with nature. I realized, as you moved, the minutes of the day
were still. When beauty walked into the room that day, the passage of
time was no longer constant. No distance will ever separate what love
is meant to be.*

Love, McKinley"

The next day I rode into town and dropped the missive off at
the hotel, and, while I wanted so much to see a smile from Lizzie
that would begin upon her lips and then settle in her heart, I had

work to do back at the house. I found myself more eager to turn the cruel life my brother had given to me into something more meaningful. I had gotten to the point where I didn't patrol the fields as I should, and, quite frankly, the slaves had become rather lazy in their efforts around the plantation. Therefore, I stood watch over nearly every tobacco leaf that was pulled, every ear of corn shucked, and every straw of hay raked—ever so conscious of securing my future.

In the weeks after that, I received three more love notes from Lizzie, and, as a way to permanently win her heart, I responded to each of them and poured my emotions onto the paper like spring rain in the middle of April. Even Edward seemed ecstatic when he read the letters to me. It was the first time in all my life I saw my brother have no contempt for me as he was the primary one to say I'd never marry. What was peculiar, though, was Lizzie's reluctance to speak of the content of the letters when I visited with her. We talked about everything under and near the sun; except for her affections. I accepted her hesitance as a form of reserved compassion, perhaps the saving of it until we were some day married. We'd taken long walks together and had shared many afternoon teas together. On numerous occasions, Lizzie resisted showing her fondness for me; particularly in the presence of others. When I tried to reach for her hand, she would pull away, and, when I tried to kiss her, she would say to me, "Not here, McKinley. Such moments as these should remain private." Respecting her wishes, I contained my emotions and withheld them for more appropriate times.

One morning I awoke to find a note from Lizzie lying next to my pillow. Katie, who lived in the house with me, had assisted me with covering the windows with dark fabric, and another of the servants repaired many of the broken shutters to help in shielding the sunlight. I'd moved from the closet to the largest of the bedrooms and was able to hear fairly well when someone entered the house. I got scantily dressed and immediately took the note to Edward. He was, again, seated in the parlor eating his breakfast. "I have another. Might you read it to me?"

Edward, sliding hominy against the prongs of his fork, mixing it with bits of sausage, displayed a demeanor of unconcern. "I'm eating, McKinley, and don't have time for that foolishness. That silly woman wants nothing from you because you have nothing. She should be told that, you know."

"Money does not make a man, McKinley, and, through her words, I know she has some sort of feelings for me."

"And that's about right, too. Some sort of feelings," he mumbled as tiny particles of food sprayed from his mouth. "What do you really know about this woman, brother? All I know is every time I see her, she's still dressed in that wretched black dress. Isn't the mourning period traditionally over by now, anyhow?"

"You, I, nor anyone else can control how long Lizzie grieves. She will come around in her own time. Can you please just read the note for me, Edward? I didn't come in here to banter with you about Lizzie's attire or her feelings which, I might add, are quite evident."

Twisting his mouth in such a way where I knew he was agitated with me, Edward snatched the letter from me seeing as though I would not leave until he had read it. Slurping the last of his coffee, he began:

"*McKinley, although the words of my mouth sometimes echo the mind of the foolish, my heart speaks the language of love in tongues only understood by the wise. My time with you may be filled with silence, but the space within which we exist is strengthened by the clamoring of ardor as it is intertwined with infatuation. Lovingly yours, Lizzie.'"*

Before the sun could stretch from one side of the earth to the other, I went to Lizzie and asked her to have my hand in marriage. The year was 1837. Since Edward decided at the last minute to take a trip to Suffolk to visit with his friend, Mills Riddick, whose house had been destroyed in a fire down there, Mavis stood up for me at the wedding, and Lizzie used little Katie in the absence of any friends or family. Lizzie, who never looked more beautiful to me, exchanged her black mourning dress, at my urging, for a wedding gown which was absent of the virgin white but embellished with bits of crystal, silk and lace. While my means tended to be that of a pauper, I managed to barter a few of the field hands for the assistance of a dressmaker in town. From the moment we emerged from the church as husband and wife, my sole purpose in life became to make my wife happy and give her only the finest money could buy.

❊❊❊

Three weeks after we'd wed, a black carriage pulled up to the main house around noon. With Edward away, there had been no visitors. Lizzie stepped into the doorway and watched as the carriage sat there seemingly waiting for someone to come out to greet it. "McKinley, is your brother expecting company?"

Walking up behind her, wrapping my arms around her waist, I answered bewilderedly, "Not that I'm aware of. Most everyone knows he's been in Suffolk the past few weeks. I'll go see who it is that's calling on him." I stepped around my wife and pulled my hat from the post in the wall. "I'll be right back." When I walked around the carriage, I could hear a bunch of commotion inside.

"Take your hands of me, nigger!" a voice yelled ferociously. Immediately, I noticed it was Edward, and he was being escorted from the carriage by its driver and a White gentleman I'd never met.

As they managed to secure Edward's composure, the man spoke, looking me from top to bottom. "You must be McKinley."

"Who's asking?"

Holding on to my brother's arm rather tightly, he continued, "I am Mills Riddick, a comrade of Edward's."

"Oh, yes, yes. Nice to make your acquaintance, sir. What is going on with my brother?" I asked, watching them tussle with an uncompromising captive.

Mills, with the assistance of the driver, tossed Edward to the ground. "Your brother," he snarled, "has been sleeping with my wife in my house, mind you, and rather than be a man and confess to it, he claims to not remember." Briskly slapping the palms of his hands together and dusting them in the direction of my brother, who seemed unaware of his actions, the man rid himself of his association with the Wellsworths. "This man here does not deserve all of this—these riches. He's not worthy of it, for he lacks the brains to guard it. You should be careful because, in his condition, someone could come in and take it right out from under your noses."

"Yes, I understand. My brother has been battling with bouts of memory loss over the past several months. I'm not sure as to why. Some days he remembers nothing, and then others he remembers too much."

"Please, McKinley, do you confuse me for a fool? A man never forgets the smell of good pussy. Once he's found his way to it, he, like a wild dog, never forgets where he has laid."

I knew Edward was likely in his right mind when he pursued Mr. Riddick's wife, but one thing he never dared admit was that his wife had to have been a willing participant and never denied him entry. "That is a likely scenario, but, as I said, my brother's mind has not been what it used to be. It doesn't excuse his actions, but it does lend a bit of sympathy, don't you think?"

Never addressing my question, Mills snubbed, "That is unfortunate. Edward's got a fine place here, and, if too many find out about his condition, they will surely try to swindle him out of it."

By now, Lizzie had made her way to where I was standing and batted her beautiful eyes at Mills. "Good day, sir. I'm Lizzie Wellsworth, McKinley's wife."

Tipping his hat, he said respectfully but hurriedly, "Riddick, Mills Riddick. Pleasure to meet you, ma'am, however, pardon me, as I intend not to be rude, but we have been traveling for days because Edward could not remember the roads back to this place. We were out of the way by many, many miles and are in desperate need of some rest."

"Might you stay here, Mr. Riddick? There is plenty of room," she offered as she looked to me for approval.

"I appreciate the gesture, ma'am, but no thank you all the same. Simber, my driver, is able to make the ride back." While the door was graciously held open for him, Mills entered the carriage and refused to look in the direction of my brother.

"Yahhh! Yahhh!" the driver ordered as he snapped the leather against the skin of the two horses. "Yahhh!" and just as quickly as they rode in, they disappeared encased in a cloud of dust. But there, on the ground, was Edward, lying as helpless as an infant.

Lizzie, never a fan of her brother-in-law, turned to Katie, who had joined us. "Go fetch Master Mavis and tell him he needs to bring a doctor with him."

❂❂❂

Early in the evening of the following day, Mavis arrived with Doctor Willingham. Lizzie and I had, for the first time, slept in the main house to watch over Edward, whose condition appeared to have worsened, for he had no recollection of his visit to Suffolk or how he got back home.

"McKinley, the doctor and I need talk with you outside a minute," Mavis requested. "Lizzie and Katie can sit in here with Edward. He's harmless right now."

My brother had been asleep most of the time and had only awakened to take in a meal or two. His servants were loyal to him and had learned how to care for him in his delicate state. They reluctantly obeyed me from time to time. I'd once asked Katie what it was he had done or said to them to make them act like they did. To my dismay, he had promised that when he died, they could each own a piece of the land, but most importantly, they could have their freedom.

The three of us walked outside in the direction of the dairy house, almost a quarter of a mile from the residence. "What is it, Mavis?"

"I'm going to let the doctor tell you," he said. It was hard to tell what Mavis's emotions were since he was pretty much the same way all the time.

"McKinley, I spent a few hours observing Edward, and his memory loss is quite astonishing," the doctor said. "He's not sure where he is most of the time, and he doesn't even know who you are."

"Surely, you jest, Doctor. Edward has taken great pleasure in knowing who I am because it is a constant reminder of who he is not." I grinned.

"I'm being as honest with you as I can possibly be. There are brief instances where he can recall simple things, but anything complex is a problem for him."

"Meaning?"

"Well, he knows the sun is bright, and he knows that grass is green. Those are simple things. But when it comes to who he is, who you are, and who his servants are, those are complexities. He quickly forgets niggers are not his equals because he allows them liberties normally not given to them. He speaks to them as if they are his friends. He doesn't see color—only what he thinks to be natural human interaction. Eventually, he will completely forget how to dress and feed himself, and he will need someone to constantly be with him to clean his urine and feces because he will not always remember where the outhouse is."

Everything Dr. Willingham was saying to me sounded like a bad dream. I had no desire to become Edward's caretaker, and I be damned if I was going to put my wife through it. "Can we not send him somewhere to die? I know that sounds cruel, but there is no place for him here."

"Send him away?" Doctor Willingham scoffed.

To protect the infinite number of ill-words formed in my brain from spewing through my lips, Mavis interrupted, "What McKinley means to say is that he and his wife will gladly take care of Edward here in surroundings that are familiar to him. It would be best if he died in the home he's worked so hard to maintain. There are enough darkies around here to carry him all the way to heaven on a one-horse cart. We'll be fine. It's getting late, Doc. Allow me to show you to the barn where they've been tending your horse," he said convincingly. Looking over his shoulder as they walked toward the main road, Mavis regulated, "McKinley, wait right here for me. I'll be back shortly."

❖❖❖

Thirty minutes later Mavis returned to find me standing against an oak tree adjacent to the dairy house. I had lit my pipe and was watching the circles of smoke vanish into the night. I'd never imagined I'd be responsible for taking care of Edward. He, for what it was worth, always took care of me, and it's no secret how that turned out. For years, he'd allowed people to spit on me and throw things at me. In spite of the fact that I was a real person with feelings, he treated me as if I were invisible, forcing me to fight for my own integrity.

"I can't believe how stupid you were about to be."

"What?" I asked.

"That man did not need to know all of that."

"Mavis, I didn't tell him anything," I said calmly. "Besides, it's no secret Edward and I are not the best of friends."

"Yes, but it is a secret that you are the actual owner of your family's fortune."

"Mavis, there's no way I can legally take all of this. I mean, the minute he comes around, he will do everything in his power to undo it."

Standing before me in utter disbelief, Mavis questioned, "Do you not understand, your brother will not recover from this?"

I wanted very badly to believe my best friend because it would mean the end of years of humiliation. "I understand whole-heartedly what is going on. I am not a complete idiot," I stated, clenching my pipe between my teeth.

"Then stop acting like one. I devised a plan to take over the plantation several years ago, but now it seems it will be easier than what I'd first thought. We will keep Edward in his bedroom, so he cannot detect any changes in his environment. Doctor Willingham said he might wander off from time to time if he's not watched, so you'd be justified in keeping him under lock and key for his own safety. You and Lizzie can move your things into your new home right away."

"What about his servants? They will…"

"They won't be able to do shit because in the morning you are going to relieve all of them of their duties and send them back out to the fields. You will replace them with servants of your own. This is your plantation now, and you can do whatever you want without asking anyone anything."

It all sounded good, but I was still not convinced. "What about the money, Mavis? You know there's money buried in the walls and underneath that house."

"Spend it. Spend it on whatever you please. Just do it wisely so as to not draw attention to you. Hell, I'm sure your wife can help you do that."

Finally, a chance to give Lizzie what she deserves, I thought. I knew she had a sizable amount of money her mother had left her, but it was hers and hers only. I never asked how much it was, nor did I ever ask for a piece of it. "Okay, Mavis, I will do it, but if anyone asks…"

Mavis was so cold and calculating sometimes that it frightened me. "If anyone asks you where your brother is, he is dead. Understand? He is dead."

13

LIZZIE
February 1859

"When beauty enters the room…"

Twenty-two years I have been married to McKinley, and I have yet to understand what, if any, affections I have ever had for him. In the beginning, it was his obvious immediate attraction to me that piqued my interest. He was able to keep my attention, and he had this way of making me feel like I was the only one in the room. Before I arrived in Hampton Roads, my mother ranted in her letters about these two gentlemen she had met. She was not that fond of the one who was a lawyer, but the other was kind and seemed to be husband material. She explained he came from money but was more like the black sheep of the family. An outcast in the community, he was in need of someone who could provide him compassion and friendship. My mother was certain that if he ever found that, then the giver of it would have all the extravagances in the world. I could not understand, however, what she meant when she said, "The love will come in due time."

McKinley's appearance was startling at first. I'd never seen anyone like him in Georgia and was not accustomed to being around someone who was different. Of course, there were the niggers who I was used to. The slave codes dictated how we treated them, and those rules were the same no matter where I went. I never want to see a day where a nigger can have the same or more than me. Then there was the issue with Will. The only person who knew about Will's sickness was Annie, and, being the type of person she was, I don't think she really gave a damn about it. While I had not cared much for him in the first place, it troubled me greatly to see a man compromise his relationship with God by doing things against His will. It was simply not natural, and it was definitely humiliating to see a man choose to slide himself into the ass of another instead of inside of me. Honestly, it was quite dreadful.

Prior to that, I'd had to deal with being what refined Southerners such as Litton and Risella Few called poor white trash. I'd lived modestly with Will, but he could not produce the lifestyle of which I yearned. When my father took up with Miss Frances, he stopped concerning himself with my upbringing and focused mainly on keeping his whore happy. She wasn't as crude as my mother, but she wasn't my mother, which gave me every reason in the world to resist her. I indulged heavily in my friendship with Annie and looked forward to any time I spent with her and her family. Compared to what means I came from, they were like royalty. Jealousy was something I wouldn't readily admit to when around my best friend, but it was indeed something I harbored. I wanted the multitudes of servants the Fews and Smiths had; I wanted the strong sense of family they shared; and I wanted to be able to experience the kind of love Annie and Royce had. Once they married, it was as if she tossed me and Will the leftovers, forcing us to live like their slaves. I knew I was worthy of the same life she had, and, upon leaving Georgia, I sought to get it. I wonder sometimes whatever happened to Annie.

As far as I knew, there was nothing to tell me how to deal with McKinley, so I blame my initial treatment of him on my ignorance. My mother was not a nice woman and was not easy to get along with; however, this man had the ability to soften her heart, and, unlike the feelings she had for most, she was extremely fond of him. I am not sure what part of his life she'd been able to delve into, but she knew quite a bit about his relationship with his brother. Sometimes I wondered, if he was such a good man, why she had not ever pursued his affections.

"My child, my life is about over, and I have grown used to being alone. It is something, however, I do not wish for you. I have set things in place to protect your future. There will be times when you may not want to follow your heart, but remember it will never lead you astray. The heart never lies."

After my mother's death, I began to notice McKinley was persistent with his emotions toward me. The letters I sent to him were to express my true feelings about him, and I was astounded by his responses to me. His words melted in my heart, for, unlike others, I knew he would never abandon his thoughts toward me. Conversations with him had always been full of surprises. On occasion, he would bring me some token of affection, like a box of candy or flowers, and present it to me just when he thought I might have lost interest in our conversations. He was a wise man; full of wit and intrigue. Since the day I met him, he had a been a delight to me because he'd been able to fill me with the kind of comfort you get when you know someone is going to always be around...no matter what. Not since Annie had anyone like that crossed my path.

Through the years, I will admit looking upon McKinley had been hard, but I tried my best to love him all the same. Twice,

I had been intimate with Will, and each time he was more involved with being inside of me than with trying to gratify me. We'd only kissed three or four times, and he knew nothing about *my* pleasure. McKinley, however, was able to hold my large breasts between his hands and pull my skin through his lips as one would a piece of meat. Pounding my walls with his huge peck, my womanhood imploded with pleasure as my eyes were closed to the beast upon me. He knew how to mash his lustful impressions into parts of my body not normally aroused, and, while I would scream passionately as my loins throbbed with heat, I would lose it the minute our eyes met, causing me to turn away in disgust. For me, Lord, it was not the act but the man. We discussed having children and hurriedly came to the conclusion that we'd have a child far less than perfect, and neither of us wanted that.

It finally got to the point where I wanted nothing from McKinley. The loneliness I endured in my short life with Will had followed me, and I wasn't aware of any way to escape it. I had walked away from one marriage, leaving behind whatever measly fortune I was due. I hadn't the intention to do that again, for the reward, in this instance, was much greater.

❋❋❋

During most of the month, Mavis and McKinley had meetings regarding traveling to Savannah for a slave auction that was to take place on the third of March. Postings about it were in the newspapers, and word about it had spread up and down the eastern coast. Since our wealth had almost doubled, I felt that we needed more help around the plantation. We'd sold off all but one of Edward's former servants because, even after whipping them down to the bone, they insisted on talking amongst themselves about his whereabouts. McKinley wanted to keep January around, though, because he was a hard worker who knew how to work all of the equipment, and he also had the respect of the other slaves. He was a little sweet on Katie, but, because she was so heavily guarded by McKinley, January kept his distance. He'd asked McKinley several times if he could marry her, and the answer was always no. But one day, McKinley, who I learned could be just as shrewd as his brother, told January he could marry her, but, if she didn't have a child within the year, he would sell her. Well, they had four children in the first four years. Little did they know, McKinley's plan was to take the children to auction when they were of age.

"McKinley?" I asked, thumbing through the *Norfolk Herald* to read about the auction in Savannah for myself. There was a huge display about it, saying there would be well over four hundred slaves for sale.

"Yes, dear," he answered as he stuffed his clothes into his travel bag.

"Is there some reason I can't go with you and Mavis on your trip to Savannah?"

McKinley never broke his stride with his packing. "No, there isn't. I figured it might be too harsh for you to experience. Nothing but a bunch of filthy niggers stinking up a barn. It could take hours to sell all of them. It's not really a place for a lady."

"But if I want to go, can I?"

"I suppose. I may need to speak with Mavis, though. We will need to take one of his carriages if another person joins us. I don't have anything large enough. You know how you tend to over pack when we travel." He laughed.

Truly, I hadn't a reason to journey to Savannah, but I knew I didn't want to stay home. Joining McKinley on the trip would give me a chance to experience another aspect of life that was typically closed to me. "I'll get my things."

❆❆❆

When Mavis arrived at the house ready to leave for the Low Country, McKinley was standing on the porch with my and his bags alongside him. January was on hand to put the baggage aboard and to drive the carriage, and Katie had a basket of fresh sandwiches for the road. "My Lord, McKinley, you sure got a ton of bags, like you plan on never coming back," Mavis hooted.

"Esquire, I'll have you know my wife will be joining us. All but one of these bags belongs to her."

I was sly about my wishes, for I knew Mavis would not go on the trip if I were going. Mavis disapproved. "McKinley, she cannot go. Women are not allowed at the auctions, and they are particularly strict about it down South."

Brushing past Mavis and extending my hand to my husband for his assistance in stepping up into the carriage, I took my seat and said, "I'm ready when you gentleman are."

Mavis peeked his head into the carriage and watched me as I opened one of the packages Katie had prepared. "McKinley, hell no. I am not riding to Savannah with your wife. Are you mad?"

My husband knew any objection to my presence was cause for an instant fight. "Mavis, we will be fine."

"How do you figure that? Look at her! She's already eating up our food. Before you know it, she's going to start nagging and…"

Cutting his eyes at me while casting me that gentle smile, letting me know everything was going to be just fine, McKinley persuaded, "Please let it be. If I don't let her go, I may not have a place to sleep when I get back."

McKinley knew I was a hell raiser. I pouted and cried when I could not have my way, and I often threw tantrums and reminded him of how he'd never find another woman who would want to be with him. Without discussing it any further, McKinley joined me inside the carriage. Mavis chose to sit in the driver's seat with January.

14

Every hotel in Savannah we got to was full, and I'd grown dreadfully restless. My bottom side was sore from the bumpy ride, and I'd grown tired of being closed up with McKinley for so long. Emotionally, we were no longer in the same place. He still adored me, but I felt more repulsed by him. I used my cunning ways to get whatever I desired from him, which included sex when I could no longer fight the urge to have my needs addressed or when my fingers had lost the sensation needed to arouse me.

❄❄❄

Two days earlier while we were traveling at undeclared speeds through South Carolina, I drifted off into a deep sleep, being exhausted from the lack of excitement. While I slept, I dreamed of warm waters cascading from my groin, and the currents washing against my inner thigh with a subtle force that rejuvenated my innocence. Writhing in pleasure, I blissfully slapped both palms against the windows of the carriage in a moment of twilight slumber as I lifted my buns from the seat. Squeezing my thighs together, the waters burst through my gates, and I awakened to find my hoops and petticoat concealing my sporadic pants and McKinley's face pressed against the split between my legs. I pushed his head into me and met him with gyrations from within. I yelped in lustful tongues until I exploded. McKinley removed himself from my lap and wiped his face with the handkerchief he always kept in his pocket. I watched him adjust himself as if nothing had ever happened.

Looking out the window as we entered the streets of Charleston, my husband's callous demeanor reminded me of why I sometimes detested him so much. He no longer knew how to touch me and extend his caresses to my heart. We passed by shops where McKinley had bought me the finest dresses and furnishings. I'd learned to not want for anything. To a degree, I'd shut him out of my world, and the one constant thing I did do for him was to keep his secret about his brother. Our money seemed endless most times; although we did little to draw attention to us. Every so often McKinley would buy me something extravagant, but Mavis always seemed to raise more hell whenever he did. "You can't do that, McKinley. You can't do it until all of *that* is dead and buried." I finally got tired of it and told him to not buy me anything. I couldn't continue to sleep at night, wondering if someone would come to the house demanding to see Edward. Heaven forbid, if Ignatius and his mother ever came to claim what was supposedly his, I'd lose it.

❋❋❋

Savannah was bursting at the seams with owners in town for the auction, which was being held at the racetrack. Despite the smell of a looming rain, the city was scenic and peaceful with majestic oak trees adorned with Spanish moss. The citizens were pleasant and quite helpful as we inquired about housing. Just beyond Forsyth Park, where the most beautiful fountain I'd ever seen stood, Mavis found a room for McKinley and me, and then he got himself one two doors down. I'm not really sure where they sent January. We had passed many, many people in the streets, but I didn't see many women.

"McKinley, I told you she would be out of place here. Females don't come to auctions. I believe she's got you hen-pecked," Mavis said.

Sometimes I felt it best to hold my tongue with Mavis because I knew I'd say unladylike things to him. I couldn't make him mad at McKinley because he was the only friend he had and was the only person between him and the family money. While he didn't spend it, he governed it. He allowed us to spend frivolously for a while, but once some of the merchants started questioning McKinley about Edward, Mavis put a lid on spending and made us live on only what was necessary.

I'd listened to his mouth for as long I could stand it. "To hell with you, Mavis. I'm here, and there isn't plenty shit you can do about it, so you may as well get used to it."

His face skipped all over pink and turned straight red. "How dare you speak to me like that? I am the reason you and your husband are where you are. You would be nothing without me."

"You think I care about that? You've held us like prisoners in that house. McKinley can't even take a pee without you knowing about it."

I knew Mavis was having his fill of me, but I didn't care. "Lizzie, I think it best we stay apart during this trip. The auction begins tomorrow afternoon, and I will see you all then." He turned to walk away.

Finally, McKinley spoke up calmly, "Mavis, wait, this is nonsense; the way you two carry on. I will speak with Lizzie, in private, if you promise to stay. I would like for you to go with us to view the lot they have for sale."

Incensed, I exclaimed, "McKinley!"

"Woman, you must learn your place and stay there," he said firmly. "I'm your husband, and the Lord says you must obey me, for I am…"

"Don't you dare, don't you dare," I scowled. I walked over to McKinley until I was able to look him in his pinkish eyes. "I will have January take me back to Williamsburg this instant, and, as sure as the Lord you speak of is my witness, I will shout from the hilltops that you truly give new meaning to the question, 'Am I my brother's keeper?' So, don't you or he fuck with me."

I didn't think McKinley could get any whiter than what he already was, but I watched his countenance turn the shade of nothingness. My temper came mostly from the lack of appropriate sleep, but it was complicated by Mavis's presence. I snatched one of my bags from the curb and slipped inside the door of the hotel, still within earshot from where Mavis and McKinley were standing.

"I warned you about her," Mavis said tersely. "I told you she was trouble."

"I love her, Mavis, and you know that," my husband attested.

"I know you do, but has it ever occurred to you that she might not love you?"

"Not once."

"My friend, I see the way you look at her, and I see the way she looks at you. Those glares are not equal."

"You see what you want to see. You don't have a love in your life and are insanely jealous of me and what I have."

"You believe I am envious of this mockery of a marriage you have? You are mistaken about that, but I do pity you, for you are a good man and deserve so much better. She doesn't want you...only money—no matter whose it is. I've never agreed with your brother about anything, but, on this, I must."

"Lizzie may be feisty most of the time, but she loves me. I've seen inside her, and I know it is true. If you have never done anything for me, please do this for me, and let her be."

Mavis paused for a moment but then followed with, "Alright, McKinley. When we get back to Virginia, I'm going to take a rest for a while from you and your wife. We have conventions coming up about this secession matter, and I will be away for several weeks."

"Secession?"

"Long story. Will talk to you about it when the time is right. Instead of going back to Williamsburg with you, I'm heading on to Richmond. From there, it's on to D.C."

"I see. Are you doing this because of..."

"It's for the greater good of the White folks in this country and nothing else, McKinley. Your wife doesn't have that kind of control over me as she does you."

❂❂❂

Contempt was not harsh enough to describe the feelings I had against Mavis. He was an ass, and there was nothing I could do or say about him when it came to my husband. We both were faced with living with one another; whether we liked it or not.

15

Slaves were crammed into the barn like bees in a hive, except there was no sweetness about the circumstances. Pouring rain kept many buyers in their hotel rooms, and even I had considered not going. The conditions in the barns were deplorable; smelling of horse manure, stale hay, and unclean human flesh. I watched as slaves tried to sell themselves to potential owners by further degrading themselves through means of which I was not accustomed. One male slave, in particular, allowed McKinley to pull open his mouth and examine his teeth and gums. Another pulled off his shirt to expose his muscular frame, which was covered with scars from previous whippings, some still healing.

"A troublemaker," McKinley leaned over and whispered to Mavis.

"Yes, he might be, but he has the body of an ox and could fetch a pretty penny back in Virginia."

"A thought," McKinley commented as he walked past and onto the next. We went about the expedition for nearly two hours before he came to the conclusion that the trip had been a waste of time. "Maybe we missed something because I, for one, don't see anything having been worth the journey or the money."

"There are over four-hundred slaves here; I know we haven't seen all of them. We haven't gone over to the other stables yet," I said.

No matter how nasty I could be at times, McKinley never mistreated me and always looked out for my well-being. "Dear, why don't you let me take you back to the hotel where you can rest? Mavis and I can finish this."

"No, I don't want to do that. I want to be here. I'm sure we'll come across something soon." We looked until sunset but to no avail.

As we were leaving, Mavis commandeered the attention of one of the many men working throughout the grounds. "Excuse me, sir, might I have a word?" I was certain Mavis was making every attempt to ignore our efforts to exit, and I had grown sick of his antics.

"Yes, sir?" The man smiled.

"My name is Mavis Crump, and these are my friends, the McKinleys. We traveled here from Virginia and are looking for bargains. I was hoping you would be able to perhaps point us in the direction of something worth our time and money."

The Southern gentleman, far from refined, stood in front of us picking at his nose and wiping his fingers across his jacket. "Mr. Crump, if I may, many of these niggers has been on the Butler place for years and don't know no diff'rent. 'Pendin' on what you wants dem fer is da only way I can offer you help."

"Forgive me, sir, but your name is?"

"Walsh. Benny Walsh. I'm the auctioneer."

"Very well then, Mr. Walsh. Any help you can give will be fine. We came too far to..."

"Lots of people comes from ferther dan you, Mr. Crump."

Obviously bothered with Mavis's questions, he rushed, "Towards the end of the auction is when we has sum of da bess ones. Dat's all I can gives you."

Mavis didn't have any choice but to take that information and sit on it.

❀❀❀

The next morning we arrived at the racetrack as the slaves were being prepared to go to what they called the Grand Stand where the auction was to be held. It seemed like the bottom was going to fall out of the sky because the rain had not stopped from the day before, and water was flowing relentlessly every- where, cascading over everything. Last minute buyers were still inspecting slaves as they exited the stables, and I, although often a compassionate person, cared less about their fates. It was adver- tised that the slaves were all from the same plantation, meaning they were related or had been together for a long time. The weep- ing sometimes was unbearable because most buyers came not with the intent to buy entire families. As they filed out, McKinley followed closely behind them so he could get to our seats.

"Lizzie, come, dear, they are about to begin," he urged gently.

"Go ahead and get our seats. I will be along shortly," I en- couraged.

Watching McKinley and Mavis as they went ahead of me, I wandered to the back of the stable where the end of the line extended. Mostly, there were only females and children in the back whose eyes were hopelessly saddened by the fate awaiting them. All of the doors to the individual stables were opened— all but one.

"Pardon me, pardon me," I tried to yell to the front of the line. "There is still a closed door back here." No one heard me because the line kept moving as the slaves were driven like cattle to the long room. "Hello? Does anyone hear me?" Still, no one returned.

The stall was in a dark corner of the barn where the rain teemed in through cracks in the roof. "Hello?" I asked anxiously, opening the door slowly. "Is anyone in there?"

There was no response, and it was difficult trying to see all the way to the back. "Hello?" Ordinarily, I would have resigned that there was no one else in there, but something within me was drawn to seeing the unknown.

"Ma'am?" a deep voice posed just as I was about to step inside. "You shouldn't be back here. All the niggers is already out dar near the platform."

Stepping backward, I stood before a scraggly man who hadn't any teeth and was dripping wet with water. Embarrassed, I smiled, "Well, sir, I thought I saw something in there. I…"

"Ma'am, deys all been 'counted fo, and we gots dem outside. Come wit me, and I'll git ya to yer seat. Fine lady lak you shudn't be in a place lak dis no ways," he grinned, extending his hand to lead me over the puddles of water.

A-choo! I looked to him, and he to me, for neither of us had sneezed. "I told you there was someone in there. I told you."

"Ma'am, gonna haff to ast ya to gwone out front and take yer seat, and letz me handle dis." Shooing me on my way, the man demanded harshly, "C'mon, outta dar, fo I has to come get ya!"

While I wanted desperately to see my discovery, I obliged the man and appeared to go out of the stable. Instead, I hid in another stall and peeped my head over the side of the wooden slats that comprised the wall. I saw an image wrapped in a dark covering emerge slowly from the doorway and extend its wrists to be chained.

"Now whar did you comez from?" he asked but didn't get an answer. His looks were more frightening than his actions as I watched him place metal bangles over both wrists and ankles and lead the stowaway to the Grand Stand.

❁❁❁

Bidding went through the afternoon and on into the late evening. Brothers and sisters had been sold from one another while most husbands and wives remained together for the purpose of breeding; especially if they were still young. I'd gotten tired of hearing the constant wailing and begged McKinley to leave, but he would not. "We will stay until they tell us to go home for the night."

"But McKinley, I am tired. We have been here all day, and you haven't even bid on anything. We shall come back tomorrow to see if they have better pickings."

"Shhh!"

As others joined my husband in his plea for my silence, I twitched and fidgeted until I felt like I was going to snatch my clothes off. Being cooped up like a wet dog had not been my idea of an enjoyable time. I was slightly concerned, though, about not having seen the stowaway but knew it would likely be the next day before they got to it. Shortly before ten in the evening, the constant buzzing and chatter was brought to an end as bidding closed for the day. The slaves were led out in the same fashion they had been brought in—chained and silent.

On the following day, Mavis and McKinley spent more time

fraternizing with the other buyers than paying attention to what was happening with the auction. He'd missed the only family that had been sold, and he ignored the applause when four wenches in a row were bought by the same slave driver. The last to be bargained was an old mammy whose first bid was for one dollar. The crowd burst into laughter as the bid grew only by ten cents at a time. Both my husband and his friend joined in the game as everyone watched. The bidding finally closed at two hundred fifty dollars. It was apparent that the auction was indeed over, but Mr. Walsh had not left the platform as I saw the scraggly man from the stable whisper something in his ear. For the first time in two days, the rain slacked, and a tiny ray of sunshine struggled to brave the clouds.

"Wait!" Mr. Walsh exclaimed. "There is but one more."

Most of all the buyers returned to their seats, including McKinley and Mavis. "How much more of this must we take?" Mavis inquired. "There surely can't be anything worth having left."

The clanks of chains never seemed louder, for it could be clearly heard over the fervent whispers of the growing crowd. Unlike the previous slaves brought into the Grand Stand, Mr. Walsh led the final item to be sold to the platform. The rain returned, splattering drops against everything in its path, but then too, the sun continued to shine. Every motion seemed slower than the last while all eyes feasted on the figure covered in burlap.

"Gents and ladies, we have one more that is not of..." And then he yanked the blanket from its body.

Everything else was a blur to me. I do not know what life was before that moment. My heart's rhythm had started over, and, despite the rain, the sun burst wide open with brilliance. Before me stood something not from this world, something too beautiful for any man to ever destroy. It was beyond beauty for me. It was something I'd never in this lifetime seen. All loves I had known, at that point, never mattered to me because it was clear to me I had never known love. There was nothing left in my soul but an absence of true love. A hush fell upon the room where, for me, passion entered.

16

PASSION
March 1859

"The hardest tears to cry are the ones no one can see."

The rain outside poured to the ground like the tears from my soul. The only difference was there was nothing to catch them. In unfamiliar surroundings, I could not afford to show any signs of weakness.

Mr. Walsh had somehow overlooked my presence when he was inspecting those who came before me. For these some twenty years of my life, I had been shielded from this cruelty and wondered desperately why this misfortune had befallen me. Like the others before me, I had done nothing to deserve this. At the back of the stables, I had heard children being torn from their mothers; sisters separated from their brothers; and wives dragged screaming from their husbands. I did not have anyone there for me to cling to. It was the first time in my life that I felt alone.

"Gal, take dat wrap off so we can see you," the auctioneer commanded.

Mother had always told me to never let a White man have to tell me more than once to do something. With my eyes fixed upon the ground below, I slowly dropped the blanket that had become my security from the environment and watched it be tossed to the ground with my dignity. My head hung low, I want-

ed so much to die at that moment, for I was about to fully surrender the freedom that had been compromised several days
before. My hair—long, straight, and black like my mother's had
been—was matted to my head with mud and sand. My eyes,
while sullen with grief and disdain, had no desire to focus on the
crowd that had now begun to enlarge with curious spectators
and prospective bidders. Surely not accustomed to the fairness
of my skin or to the straightness of my hair, the constant chatter
of the crowd gradually began to cease as I took to the auction
block with my ankles and hands still shackled.

"Gentlemen, here we have a nigger wench. She is sold fer no
fault. A fugitive, she has no rightful owner and is of no relation
to the lot from the Butler plantation. She was found 'longside
the river. Her age is 'round twenty-two or twenty-three. What
is your offer? Examine her. Fine fer breedin', she is. Raise your
head, gal."

I slowly lifted my head and looked out into the crowd through
my partitioned hair. Before me stood more White men than I
had ever seen. My composure began to tremble with fear.
Amazed by the continued silence, the auctioneer walked over
to the edge of the stage, picked up a bucket of standing water
and threw it against my face. Chucking the bucket off to the
side, he gently requested, "Gal, move your hair from your eyes
so the folks can see you."

Raising my chained wrists to my face, I took the back of my
hands and moved the separated strands to the sides of my head,
revealing my blue eyes.

"Two-hundred!" someone yelled.

Balking at the offer, Mr. Walsh walked over to me and grabbed
my chin with his rough, dry hands. Looking me dead in the eye
with a lustful glare, he said softly, "If I had the money, I'd buy

you for myself, but I know I'm 'bout to fetch a pretty penny fer you."

Then he snatched the front of my dress, ripping it from the top to just above the waist. As he stood in front of me before exposing me to the crowd, he shook his head in awe. I had seen many slaves before me who had scars from whippings, but I had none.

Seeing this, Mr. Walsh shouted, "Five-hundred dollars!"

Almost instantly, a frenzy started and the once silent gathering turned into the event that was to further change my life. "Five-hundred dollars! Do I hear five-hundred dollars?"

"Five-hundred," a raspy voice declared from somewhere in the middle of the room. Wearing a straw hat and a pair of mud-drenched overalls, a large man raised his hand, acknowledging his offer.

"Five-hundred dollars from the gentleman over here. Do I hear five-hundred and fifty?" Mr. Walsh spun me around, displaying the smoothness of the skin on my back. Something I had surmised while watching and listening to the sale was that the auctioneer was in charge of the room and could do whatever he wanted to do, including change the asking price when he had determined that a slave could fetch a higher price. As he glided his hands across my back, I felt filthier than the dirt underneath my feet, and the feeling heightened when he slid his finger down my spine. Leaning into me as the crowd watched him continue to molest my body before their eyes, Mr. Walsh asked, "Gal, you done had cherrin?"

"No, suh," I answered softly.

"One-thousand dollars!" Mr. Walsh bellowed. "This is an undamaged good. Do I hear one-thousand dollars?"

"One thousand one hundred!" someone offered.

Then another, "One thousand two hundred!"

Mr. Walsh kept up with the bids like he was counting money. "Do I hear one thousand three hundred?"

A strange looking man, somewhere on the front row, tipped his hat toward Mr. Walsh. "One thousand three hundred, for the gentleman down front."

"Now, do I hear one thousand four hundred? This piece of property ain't something you see every day."

All of the bustling about seemed to slow down. The bidding had reached a number that most of the gentlemen traders could not even count to. The bantering had died down, and it was apparent the bidding was about to end. Someone was about to own me and my soul for one thousand three hundred dollars.

Mr. Walsh, taking his handkerchief from his trouser pocket, blew his nose into his palms before proceeding. The rain had taken its toll on everyone in some sort of way. Steady streams of water flowed from the roof into overflowing puddles on the stable floor. The garments of the fancy gentleman who had offered the highest price were soaked, and, he, as many others, was ready to bring an end to the spectacle. At that point, the only thing that mattered to me was being able to walk from the stand into the care of someone who was, at the least, human.

"One thousand seven hundred and fifty dollars." Silence drifted across the room again because the words fell from the lips of a woman who had come with the gentleman from Virginia—the man who had offered the one thousand-three hundred dollars. Mr. Walsh wiped his forehead with his handkerchief, tapping the wrinkles above his brow. Someone had offered the highest price paid for a piece of property.

"One thousand seven hundred and fifty dollars?" he asked, astonished.

The woman, confidently displaying that she was fully aware of her offer, nodded in approval.

"One thousand seven hundred and fifty dollars from the lady," he said, clearing his throat. "Do I hear one thousand eight hundred?"

Mr. Walsh picked up my blanket, my belongings they'd found with me, and the remnants of my clothing and placed them in the chair beside the platform, awaiting another bid, but not one came. He looked around and noticed folks beginning to leave, and he quickly made the decision to bring it all to an end. "Sold for one thousand seven hundred and fifty dollars, to the fine lady from Virginia."

17

The room disassembled quickly as I was led from the platform to the foreground where my new missus was waiting. My eyes, fixed upon the ground, shifted from the chains on my ankles to the ones around my wrists. The rain outside had stopped as had the wails of the suffering broken-hearted, for each soul had gone off with its new owner. I found no comfort in knowing that my journey, while the running had ceased, had only just begun.

❁❁❁

That night, when my mother's husband fired upon me, I had to quickly consider before the bullet pierced my flesh where and how I wanted my life to end. In that same instant, I recalled Maynard's words to me about landing like a cat, so I jumped to my freedom. Never looking up to see if Royce was peeking over the cliff to see if I had been destroyed, I entered the river and swam until my arms tired from fighting with the currents. To me, there was no time to wonder what or if someone was behind me. Mother and Maynard had always told me to run and that looking back would slow me down. Having never been more than a mile or so from the cave, I ventured into land I was unaware existed. Three days came and went with me running along the banks of the river. I had managed to avoid humans, but I had grown extremely weary. As the sun set, I found a spot and spread my cape against the earth and rested. The night was indeed cold, but it protected from those I thought only preyed during the day.

"Don't-cha move, nigger, or else-n I'll blow yer brains clear out from da skull," a high-pitched male voice snarled with the barrel of his rifle pressed against my head. As I began to understand the fact my days on the run had finally come to an end, a medium-sized dog stood over me, barking into my face. When he saw I was not a threat to him, the four-legged creature came closer to me and familiarized himself with my scent, intermittently licking my face and ears.

"Git back, Jugs," he ordered, but the dog continued thrashing his tongue against my skin. "That's strange, he don't usually take too kindly to niggers. Git up, gal."

"Yessuh," I mumbled.

"Whar you from and whar yer papers at? Niggers all by demselves s'pose-n to have papers from dey master."

I did not know what I was expected to say. I had never had a master. "Suh?"

"Yer papers, you dum tramp. Gimme dat sak of yers," he demanded, putting his gun down. I handed the bag to him and watched as he violated the bond of my mother and me. Tossing each precious thing aside, he came across the gold trinket box. "Well, lookie, here. Wuts dis?"

To protect every piece of her, I spoke up, "A gift, suh, from my missus, suh."

"A gift? Look-n lak you stole it to me. I'll jes keep it wit me for safe keepin' 'til we gits bak to town," he said, sticking the box in his pocket while still digging through the bag. Far as I knew, there was nothing else in there, but he continued searching until he pulled a folded piece of paper from the very bottom. He opened the paper and started reading. "Sez you belon' to da Fews. Is dat right, gal?"

Mother. "Yessuh, I does."

It seemed he had been satisfied with my answers, and I was all too grateful to not have to speak anymore. "Well, wut're you derin' out here?"

"I comes down here for a walk and pick muscadines for my massa." Prayerfully, I watched his every move to see if he had caught me in a lie. As it seemed he was still looking over the papers Mother had apparently hidden in my bag, I felt eyes prowling about my body. If I ran, he would surely pick up his rifle.

"Now, gal, you knowed I know you's tellin' me a lie, and 'round dees parts, niggers die fer lyin'," he said as he put the paper back into the bag. "Purdy thang lak you can have anything I got long az nobody else knowed 'bout it. Dat kin include yer freedom if-n you does wut I tell you."

"Yessuh," I answered with my eyes upon his fingers as they unfastened his belt and unzipped his pants, exposing a piece of him that stood out like a pole.

"Put yer purdy lips 'round dis and suck on it 'til I tellz you to stop."

With no reluctance, I did as I was told, dropping to my knees. I put my mouth around him and pulled his peck until it stretched even longer. The wetness of my mouth provided a shield between me and him that would secure my freedom. I looked up and saw that he had not his eyes upon me but toward the sky. Pumping in and out of my mouth, I gripped him even tighter and pulled his pants down around his ankles. I reached my hand into his pocket and took back my trinket box, placing it back into the bag with all the other items I gathered from around him. Grabbing the backs of his hairy calves and thighs as I slithered up the lower part of his body, I realized the power within my lips and tongue that did not involve words. I felt his peck stiffen as if it were full of lightning. I could taste something more than me in my mouth, and then I knew it was time. I clamped my teeth around his dick, puncturing it until the skin broke and I tasted blood. He could not stop his explosion but pulled helplessly at my head to stop my desecration of him. My mouth full of blood, I wished not to swallow, so I released myself and spat into the ground. Speechless, he fell to the ground as Jugs stood by and watched.

The speed of my stride amazed me. I ran until I had to stop to catch my breath. The brisk air was pushing itself down my throat and had lodged itself in my stomach, causing a pain I could not take while still on my feet. Mother and Maynard had never told me about the slave patrols that eventually caught me and sold me to the auctioneer, who was also a slave trader.

❂❂❂

"Here," the missus said, forcing a crumpled piece of cloth into my hand. It smelled faintly of perfume.

"I am Lizzie Wellsworth, and this is yer master, McKinley Wellsworth. I'll get yer clothes. That other idiot you see is Master

Mavis Crump." She walked over to the chair where Mr. Walsh had thrown my clothing and brought the items back to me. "Get dressed," she ordered as she threw my tattered rags to the ground.

My new master came over to me with a ring of keys and lifted my wrists to unlock my chains. "I don't know what she was thinking," he said tenderly. "You can't do nothing with these things on you."

Tears streamed from my soul as I heard the click of the lock. "Thank you, suh," I mocked.

Just as I began to slide my hands through the rusted metal braces, the missus approached. "What are you doing, McKinley? Leave them on her," she said angrily.

Master, looking at every part of my exposed body, continued his efforts to release me. "Lizzie, how you expect her to get dressed? She isn't going anywhere with all these folks standing around. I'll put the chains back on after she's gotten dressed."

God knows I wanted to run, but where would I go? Those people had sat before me like a pack of hungry wolves waiting to devour me, and, if someone did not steal me first, I would have only been returned to the Wellsworths.

18

Life on the plantation was not as I had imagined. I had overheard slaves at the auction talk of their lives on the Butler plantation where they were treated like family. I wondered how that could be so when this man who thought of them as family sold them all, and I am certain he never shed a single tear about it. While I was burdened with my own torment, I sympathized with their pain. Some would leave the stables, embracing their loved ones, and then return later holding on to only their memory. Any man willing to let another feel that way was no better than the devil himself.

Immediate allies of mine were Katie and January. At first I feared January because he never talked and never smiled. When we arrived at the main house, Katie greeted Missus and Master with hot, fresh food. I was not sure I was to partake, so I stood back and awaited my instructions. January got down and began unloading the bags but never took any food. "January, be sure to get all the bags inside before you two carry on," Master said. "And Katie, this here is… Well, we don't even know your name. What they call you?"

"It is…" I began.

Missus, who stopped dead in her tracks when I opened my

mouth, jumped in, "Her name is Passion. Nothing else before now matters."

"Lizzie, what are you doing? You can't expect us to call her that."

As she bit into a warm corn muffin, she said, "One thing you seemed to have forgotten is that it was my money that paid for her—not yours. She will be called whatever I wish her to be called."

Putting forth no argument, Master continued, "Very well then. January, take Passion's bag out to…"

"He will do no such thing. She's to be placed in our old house. I want her close to me."

"Lizzie, I have asked you repeatedly if January and Katie could be put in there, and you have repeatedly told me no."

"And my answer has not changed."

January, Katie, and I watched as they went back and forth about the matter until Master conceded, and I was put in the house next to theirs.

❁❁❁

Later that night, Katie came to the house to help me clean. She brought her youngest son, Adam, with her. "You doesn't mine me bringin' him wid me, do ya? I kin…"

In the beginning, I didn't speak much, in fear of someone discovering my level of intellect. It was difficult for me to be someone I was not used to being, but I did my best. "It's awright."

Most would have likely looked around to notice the surroundings, but I could tell Katie was already familiar with the place. "Missus and Marse sho' makin' a fuss 'bout you."

"Is somethin' wrong with that?"

"No, no, jes seems strange 'coss Missus don't pays us no mind most da time."

Katie put the baby down on the floor with his blanket and got a broom from the closet. "You been out here before? You know where everything is."

"Yes, dey lived out here 'fo dey moved into da house. Marse Edward made dem stay out here."

"Who is Marse Edward?"

"Dat's Marse McKinley's brudda. He…"

"He what?"

Noticeably uneasy, Katie asked, "Whar is it you comes from? You talked plenty propah fer a nigger."

Uncertain as to what was safe to mention, I replied, "I comes from a place down South. That's the best I can tell you."

With her eyebrows turning in toward the middle of her face, she asked, "Does Missus knowed you talks lak dat?"

"No, because we have not talked. Why do you ask?"

"Beddah makes sho' she don't. She don't laks us niggers seemin' beddah dan hur," she warned as she busied herself with sweeping the cobwebs from the corners. I walked over to Adam and picked him up from the floor. I struggled for a moment because I had never held a baby before. Katie quickly noticed my frustration. "Where's ya from—a nigger dat knowed how to holes a baby?"

"I told you I'm from down South. So, you're married to January?"

Instantly, her somewhat melancholy expression turned into a pretty smile. "Yes, us is married. Bin married a good whiles. You has a husband?"

"No, I've never been married."

"Got cherrin?"

"No, I don't," I answered quickly as I turned to make up my bed. "I think I'm ready to go to bed now, if you don't mind."

Katie did not seem annoyed by my abrupt rudeness. "Dat's fine. I sees you in da mornin' win I comes up to da house to gits brekfas."

No one had given me any instructions thus far, and I surely did not want to be caught doing nothing. "What time should I be ready then?"

As she held the baby in her arms and rocked him to sleep, Katie said, "The bell sounds at dawn. Us is 'pected to be in da fields and in da house by den. Beddah not be late eder 'coss Marse don't laks dat. Us gets ten lashes if us is late."

"I'll make sure I'm ready."

Before she and Adam disappeared into the night, Katie turned to me and said, "Beddah be careful 'roun da Missus. She kin be nasty to us and to Marse sumtimes."

"Thank you for telling me." I wanted to tell her I did not trust any White person but my mother, but that was something I was not ready to share with the world. I laid wide awake my first night in my new home; afraid to close to my eyes. I knew nothing about the world around me, other than the fact I did not want to be in it. I missed Maynard, Susie, Ina, and Mother.

❂❂❂

The next morning I stepped outside the house and saw servants running from place to place, and the sun had yet to show its face. January was in the backyard chopping wood, and Katie, dressed in a long, gray gingham dress, was hurrying from the dairy house with butter in one hand and carrying a bucket of milk in the other. "Mornin', Pashin."

"Morning, Katie. Why is everyone up so early?"

"Us is always in a hurry 'round here. Da sooner we gits dun wid our chores da sooner we can gits bak to our cherrin."

"Katie!" Missus was calling her from the back of the house. "You better get in this house and get breakfast ready, and I mean right now!" I did not want Katie in trouble on my behalf, but I realized she had not waited for me to say another word and had vanished. I saw her next walking into the back door of the house and closing the door behind her. "I see you're up with the rest of them."

"Yessum."

"Good. I've always needed a good house nigger to look after me—not the house but me. Come with me."

I walked through the house with Missus and noticed the beauty of its holdings. It was the first time I had ever seen what I had only read about. We went from room to room as she ran through a list of chores I was to have. Compared to the others, my duties were minimal, for she had me doing only those things particular to her. Each morning I was expected to have her bath drawn for her; her clothes prepared; her plate fixed and sitting on the table at every meal; her tea poured at two o'clock; and her hair brushed one hundred times every night. Then, of course, I had to draw her bath at night. It was also my responsibility to dress and undress her; no matter the occasion. If Master asked me to do anything, he had to ask Missus first.

19

MCKINLEY
March 1861

Mavis came back to Williamsburg after having been gone on and off for nearly two years and told Lizzie and me about some of the Southern states seceding from the Union. There was a convention taking place in Richmond where meetings were held to discuss the possible secession of Virginia. Mavis served on the Committee on Federal Relations and helped draft a report that was eventually amended and ratified by the convention on how the state would perhaps handle future dealings with the United States. Since the election of President Lincoln, there had been talk of freeing the slaves, and I, along with other planters, did not want to see that happen. It would mean the end of life as we knew it with no one to work our land, but most importantly, niggers would be able to live as we did. With politicians battling daily over the matter, we were all impatient. A month later, on the twelfth of April, the Union attacked Confederate forces at Fort Sumter in South Carolina, and our country was officially at war. Five days after that, we got word that Virginia had seceded.

After first talking with Mavis and then Lizzie, I thought it time to have a meeting with the servants. I sent January to gather them in the courtyard. I had never seen them all at one time—

in one place, and I will admit their presence was a bit over-whelming. Once January told me everyone had arrived, I asked Lizzie to join me.

"I know you all are aware of the war that's going on about whether or not you should be free, and I felt like it was time to talk to you about your places here." My sight was near gone, therefore I relied heavily on January to make sure I knew where I was going. "The Union is nothing but a group of agitators try-ing to take over all the great things us Southerners have done to make this land profitable, and I be damned if I let them come in here and take what my family has worked so hard to create. Y'all got food, you got clothes on your back, and I make sure you got adequate quarters. If you feel like you're being mistreated, then, by all means, runaway. Remember the rule still applies that if you're caught and brought back here, then it's one hundred lashes. I might not be able to see as I used to, but I'll still do my best to skin you alive." They disbursed with a clear understanding of their fates.

❃❃❃

Edward had been kept in his room for over twenty years. Katie looked after him for me, and every so often I would stick my head in there to put my hand over his nose and mouth to see if he was still breathing. His eyes were fixed on the ceiling and rarely, if ever, shifted. I wanted so many times to take one of his pillows and press it against his face until I knew he was gone. While I'd killed before without a conscience, I did not know if I would be able to live with myself with the blood of my brother on my hands. One afternoon, while I was in his room, Edward starting coughing uncontrollably. I called out to

Katie, but she did not answer. I began going through his night-stand to find a towel to clear the mucus from his mouth. Not able to find one, I pulled back his covers in hopes that one was lost in his sheets. Still, I did not find anything. I then moved his pillows and felt about them until I discovered a slight bump in one. Taking the covering from the pillow, I traced my fingers across the imperfections and came upon stitches sewn into it. Ripping open the stitching, I stuck my hand inside and found several pieces of folded paper. I smelled them and recognized Lizzie's fragrance. Elated with my discovery, I removed the bundle and put my glasses on to try to make out the words so I could once again experience the love that brought Lizzie and me together. Barely able to see the letters, I struggled to make out the words, but I did not recollect them all They were not at all the words I remembered.

"Massa, suh?"

It was Passion; I was unaware she knew where I was. "What are you doing up here? Who told you about this room?" I demanded.

"Nobody, suh. I heard you callin' fer Katie, and I comes to tell ya she was not in da house."

"Oh, oh, alright then. I'm sorry." I had kept my distance from Passion because she belonged to Lizzie and was kept busy all the time. My, oh, my, she was a beautiful girl—more gorgeous than any nigger I had ever seen. I bid on her that day and never expected to be outbid by my own wife. Sometimes I felt that Lizzie no longer loved me, but because I knew how hard it was for someone to love me, I was committed to making it work and to keeping her happy. "Where's Miss Lizzie?" I was going to ask her to read the letters to me.

"She's restin', suh. Said she had a headache. Is there somethin' I can get fer you, suh, 'til Katie gets back?"

On the rare occasions I'd heard Passion speak, I noticed an oddity in her I had not seen in the other servants. "Passion, where is it that you came from?" The gal had nothing to say for a moment. She was afraid. "Don't worry. It's just me and you in here." Still she said nothing. Any other servant would have felt my back hand by then, but I couldn't do that to her. "Do you come from a horrid place? Please feel you can trust me."

"I came from Augusta, suh. My name was Amelia." Simply listening to her, I knew she could do something that, outside my presence, could have her killed, but I was desperate.

Opening one of the letters, I placed one of them in her hand as she stood before me. I got up and closed the door. "Please read that to me." I held her hands in mine to stop the trembling I felt. "Don't worry. It will be our secret."

The first letter read:

"McKinley, I wish that you would stop following me. I enjoy our conversations, but you are such a buffoon. I am trying to like your presence, but it sickens me to see you sometimes. The sight of you..." she read.

"Please stop," I asked, softly taking the paper from her and handing her another. "Read this one for me."

"McKinley, please stop coming to see me. I want nothing more than for us to part ways so I can find the right love for my life. You are not what my heart desires. Many desire me but will not have me because you are always around. I feel the world will hate me if I am seen trying to show you any love. You..." Passion read.

"Stop," I requested as tears flowed from my eyes. It did not matter to me that a servant had seen my weakness, nor did it matter to me that she knew how to read. What did matter was that my brother had deceived me and that my marriage had been based upon a lie. Passion, who, before I knew it had become my strength, pressed my head against her lap and allowed me to suffer privately for my stupidity.

❁❁❁

The very next day Edward died. Maybe he was holding on until I was able to discover his secret to finally let me see that he would always win and that he was right about Lizzie. I told January to build a simple pine box for him and to put my brother's body in it. He was instructed to bury him in the cemetery, and it was not necessary for him to tell me when he had finished. Most of my life had been empty of emotion for Edward, and things had finally come full circle. I wanted nothing more than to rid the world of him without inconveniencing anyone. Later in the day, Passion walked out to the tobacco fields as I sat upon my horse watching the servants work the land. "Master, I brought a cool drink for you."

I looked down from my horse while she stood there extending a glass of lemonade to me. "Where's Lizzie? I wouldn't want you to get into any trouble."

"Taking a nap, as usual," she said, handing the glass to me.

While it was beneath me to even consider the idea, I proceeded with what my heart told me to do. "Passion, I am sorry about yesterday. I should not have put you in that position."

"Master, I did as you told me to do. That's all." January was the only person who knew I could see barely what was directly in front of me, but I sat on that horse like I could see across the entire land.

"Well, thank you. It meant a lot because you read to me what my heart has felt for quite some time. My wife has never loved me, and I have been forsaken all these years. Had you not been in the room, I would have lived my whole life in a treacherous lie."

"You're welcome, sir."

Again, I listened to her speech and was slightly disturbed by it. She spoke better than any White person I knew. To attest to my gratefulness to her, I allowed her to keep that secret.

20

PASSION
April 1862

At the break of dawn I could hear the blasts of the cannons as the fighting moved closer into the Peninsula. On his way to the main house, January stopped in to check on me. He was the husband of my best friend, and she would die if she knew there had been a time or two when I could not help myself and when he did what men folk do. I can't say I liked it much, but I learned how the heart of a man works. He came to me on a day, about three months ago, when Missus had laid into me about her clothes not being pressed the way she wanted them, and I was crying in the kitchen. For him, he and Katie had been fussing about her always being up under Master. I told him he had no right feeling like that because he had been smelling around behind me for months.

"You wanna take a walk with me, Miss Passion? You needs to get 'way from dis place 'fo dees folks drives you crazy. We won't bees gone long." January and I walked down through the woods along a path Master had created for going back and forth to town. When we got to the biggest oak tree out there, I stopped and squatted to stretch my knees. January, with his hands in his pockets, stared up into the sun. "Itz nice to be 'way from all dat noys."

"Yes, it is," I said, walking over to the tree. Always tending to

Missus, I never had time to do anything for myself. "Sometimes a woman needs time just for herself," I said softly.

"Wut-cha say, Miss Passion?"

Raising my voice slightly, I repeated, "Sometimes a woman needs time just for herself. My mother used to say that whenever she would leave the cave where I was raised."

"You wus raised in a cave?"

"Yes, down in Georgia. My mother hid me from her husband, and she and some other servants raised me out there. For over twenty years, I lived like that. Mother taught me how to read and write, and Maynard, Susie, and Ina showed me how to survive."

"Whar dey et now?"

"Dead, I guess. My mother's husband discovered us, and he killed her. I do not know what happened to the others."

"No wunda you seems so sad sumtimes."

"You know, January, I am really not all that sad about that because I feel like there is still a part of me out there somewhere. That bag I keep in the corner of the house is a bag of precious things my mother gave to me. If anything ever happened to it, then I would feel truly alone."

As we were in the midst of February, the sun was bursting through the limbs of the trees, which only a few months before had succumbed to the first breath of winter. There were tiny green buds on the branches, signifying the expected presence of spring. I did not go to the woods with the intent of what happened next, but January, who was, indeed, a handsome man with large hands made me not think as I should have. His skin, the color of trodden dirt in the springtime, was rough from long hours spent in the sun and from time spent toiling until his skin was frostbitten. No words between us were spoken, and, again, I used a power from within to nourish my soul. Gently, I reached for the opening at the top of his shirt and ran my fingers along the buttons until I reached its end. I pulled it from his trousers with the bottom of it damp from his moisture. I stuck my hand inside and wrapped my hand around the thing that made him a man. January pulled me to him and pushed his lips against mine. Our tongues entangled, we exchanged our betrayal of Katie and buried it while he worked to bury himself in me. The hem of my dress was pulled to my waist as January's thrusts caused my back to rub into the bark of the tree. I grabbed his shoulders and held him close with my legs wrapped around his waist and crossed at the ankles.

❖❖❖

"Mornin', Miss Passion."

"Mornin' to you. What can I do you for?"

"Kadie ast me to stop in to see if-n you wus aw-right. I knowed you heared the cannins cus we heared dem whar we wus."

"Yes, I heard them. How long you think before it gets close to us?"

"I not sho'. Marse Mavis come lass nigh to tell Marse to be ready to move outta here if dey gets too close. 'Spectin' dey's over in Yurktown."

"January, how much do you know about Master Mavis?" I asked. I had seen him only a few times, but I knew he meant a lot to Master McKinley.

"He don't lak niggers at all. Sum uh da White mens used to comes by here and haffs our womins, but he ain't nevah did nuttin' lak dat far as I knowed."

"I see. He stays away a lot, huh?"

"Yeh, he work all da time. Ain't nevah tooked a wife. He don't laks da missus, eitha."

Chuckling, I commented, "Well, I know that. She doesn't like him either. How you and Katie doing?"

"Us is good, Miss Passion. Wurkin' hard, tryin' to keep thangs togedder."

For as long as I had known the two of them, their marriage appeared solid. "Why you have to work so hard at that? You two are happy every time I see you."

January got up and went to the door. He looked all through the front yard and the courtyard to see if anyone was around. Then he came back to where I was sitting at the table and took a seat next to me. "Marse bees really hard on hur sumtimes, makin' it real hard fer me to be da man I s'pose to be."

"What do you mean, January? You think Master's been messin' with her?"

"I thank so, and I ast hur, but she say it ain't true."

"Why don't you believe her?"

"I jes doesn't. I kin't say why neetha."

Master McKinley and I had developed a bond highly unusual for a servant and her master. At night when Missus had gone to bed, he would come to my house and talk with me about his life, the land, and just him. I never said much, and he never asked me anything. One thing he did tell me was that he always thought Katie was his daughter but refused to tell his wife that. He also said he had killed the man Katie knew to be her father, and, because he had betrayed his loyalty by running away, he felt God forgave him for it. "I think you're mistaken about that. Master would never do such a thing."

"Marses kin do whateva dey want. Dat lass chile uh ours. I ain't sho' dat's mine."

"Adam?"

"Yeh, dat's not my chile. I feel it in my heart."

Shocked by January's accusation, I said, "I think you need to trust your wife more. She really loves you. She tells me that all the time."

"I knowed she does, but... Jes nevah mine. I got to git on to work 'fo Marse comes lookin' fer me."

By late morning, Master, for what I heard was the first time he had ever done so, suspended work in the fields. "The fighting is getting too close to us, and I need to move my family out of here. You..." Then, it started. You could hear the thunder of the horses' hooves pounding the earth. Next, just below the landing, clouds of dust encased the heads of a small troop clearly visible as the Confederate Army with its flag proudly blowing in the wind. The face of its leader was one I had not forgotten. We all stood frozen in time.

"Good day, sir. I am Major General Royce Smith, and we are traveling east to meet up with another unit up nears Yorktown. Seems as we happened upon your place, might you have some water or food for us since we are fighting for the cause of keeping the niggers in their rightful place?"

Master, who I had heard, had not a kind bone in his body when it came to his servants, replied, "We have some pork in the smokehouse you might take with you, and you can have all the water you want so long as you promise to protect this place should the skirmish get up to here."

Royce, whose demeanor had not changed since the last time I saw him, agreed. "You have yourself a deal, sir."

"January, go fetch these gentlemen a pig from the smokehouse and then get one of the others to bring them some water. Also get Katie to make them some of those peach tea biscuits of hers."

I stood on the other side of Master's horse and delicately stepped out of sight. My nerves caused me to feel like the world was spinning; my gut turned sour and up came my breakfast. I made my way to the kitchen and found the missus standing in there. "Where have you been and what's all that commotion outside?" she asked as she was one to not come outside too often. When I smelled the tea biscuits baking, I felt sickly and ran outside to empty my belly again. Katie always spoke up for me when she knew I could be in trouble.

"Ma'am, Miss Passion was out in da ize house gittin' ize fer ya wauder. Dem is some soljers out dare lookin' fer food and wauder." Missus seemed to never realize I refused to hold conversations with her.

"Soldiers? Where?"

"Out in the courtyard with Marse," Katie responded.

❁❁❁

Missus ran to the mirror to check her appearance. "Passion, go get my brush and fix my hair. Then find me another dress to put on."

"Yessum," I answered quickly. I bustled through the house until I had gathered the items she requested. I pulled out a dress she had worn two days before, and, because she was in such a rush, Missus did not even notice it. Katie helped me to clothe her. It was a sad case, for she acted as an infant and, since the acquisition of my service, she had not the desire to do anything for herself. The only thing I did not do was accompany her to the outhouse.

"Passion, I'm going out to the courtyard to assist my husband with welcoming our guests. You should come, in case I need something."

"Yessum." What was I to do? I had not shared with anyone my circumstances, and Royce, should he see me, will tell them everything. "Ma'am?"

"What is it, gal?"

"Kin I help Katie wid da food? Itz an awful lot fer hur to do by hurself."

Impressing folks she did not know was a hobby of hers, and since they were battling to keep the slaves in bondage, I knew she would be willing to do anything. "Very well, but you need to hurry."

When I saw Missus had made her way from the house, I ran thoughts through my head that I felt it was the time to share. "Katie, you remember when you asked me where I came from?"

Giggling as she poured the batter into the pans, she said, "Yeh, I does. You won't gives me no answer."

"That man out there was married to my mother—a White woman by the name of Annie Few Smith. My father was Josiah—a Negro my mother's mother raised. I was raised in a cave at the edge of the plantation where my mother taught me things I would be killed for knowing. That man—that horrible man—surely believes he killed me, and if he discovers I am still alive, no war on this earth will be more important than destroying me."

"So how did you end up with the missus?"

"After I got away from him, I ran as fast as I could until the slave patrol caught me and sold me to the auctioneer."

Katie had put her things down. "If the missus fine out you kin read, I doesn't know wut she might do to you."

"Please don't tell her. I beg you."

"Miss Passion, us is friends and won't thank uh derrin' sumthin' laks dat to you." Just then January came into the kitchen with the pig.

"Iz dose muffins ready? Dey iz 'bout to leave." We closed the door behind him to tell him of my dilemma.

21

LIZZIE

I trotted to the courtyard so I would not miss any prospects. "Good day, gentlemen. I... Well, my Lord, Royce Smith!"

"Lisbeth Brown?" he gasped.

"No, no, no. It's Wellsworth now. Lizzie Wellsworth. This is my husband, McKinley Wellsworth, the owner of this land." I am quite sure he need not be reminded whose land it was, but it was ever so important to me that he see how well I had done for myself to be no longer in need of renting land from someone else.

"We've met, and he's been mighty generous by providing us with some food. We're about to be on our way, however. How long you been in this area?"

"We've been married twenty-five years, give or take a month or two. How's Annie?"

Royce's face turned lily white. "Annie is where Annie needs to be." Pausing for a moment as he looked over all of our servants still gathered in the courtyard, he asked, "Are these all your niggers here?"

"Well, yes, they are," McKinley interrupted.

"I need about twenty of them, including that one right there," he said, pointing at January as he and Katie headed toward us with the cured pig in his arms.

"You can have the others, but you can't have him. He helps me around here, and I rely on him too much to have him gone."

Royce dismounted his horse and took off his gloves. He stuck them underneath his armpit and folded his arms across the front of him. "Now, Mr. Wellsworth, what shall you do if the North wins this fight? That nigger won't have to do a damn thang for you, now will he?"

McKinley had every chance in the world to stand up to Royce. He looked at Katie, and the tears that had formed in her eyes. "Take him."

"Nooo! Nooo! Marse, pleez don't let dem take my man! Oh, Lord, pleez...!" Throwing the biscuits she cooked to the ground, Katie ran to embrace January, but no sooner than she got her arms around him, Royce ordered his men to restrain her. When they let her go, she turned to Passion for comfort.

"Alright you, darkies. Gimme twenty of you, if you can count. Ain't no time for no long good-byes and all that shit. Get your asses together and let's go."

❁❁❁

That afternoon, while waiting in the parlor waiting for Passion to bring me my tea, I realized it was taking her longer than usual. I'd never had to call for her, and I was growing impatient. "Passion, you know it is time for me to take tea," I scolded. I waited a few more minutes, but there was still no sign of her. "Passion!"

The coffee table had been set with the teapot, teacups, and peach tea biscuits. I was merely missing someone to pour. I arose from my chair, walked past the front door, spotted Passion in the garden talking to Katie. I walked to the window closest to the front entrance and did my best to hear their conversation.

"Are you eavesdropping, Lizzie?" McKinley startled me.

"Well, no, I'm not. It's time for me to take tea, and Passion should be in here pouring it for me."

"Pouring it for you? Can't you do that for yourself? She already waits on you hand and foot."

"And that's what I bought her for. Are you jealous, McKinley?"

"Not the least bit. I am, however, in need of a moment of your time. You and I are overdue for a conversation."

"We can do that after I have my tea."

Furious, McKinley yelled, "Fuck your damn tea, woman! You will sit down and talk with me this instant, or I shall find every way possible to exclude you from my life!"

"What?"

McKinley pulled a bundle of papers from his pocket and threw them at me. "I found these sewn into my brother's pillows."

I picked them up and glanced through the wording. "You already knew how I felt so why are you so angry?"

"My dear brother didn't read to me what you wrote. Instead, he read what he wanted me to hear. I know, for a fact, you have never loved me the way I have loved you."

I casually moved away from the window so as to keep our conversation private. "Once upon a time, I did love you. I don't think I've ever been in love with you, but I can honestly say I loved you very deeply."

"So you're saying you don't love me anymore?"

"Well, yes, I guess that's what I'm saying, but don't even think of asking me to leave."

McKinley couldn't expect me to have feelings for him after

all our years of discontent. "I don't know what to say, Lizzie. I have given you everything, and you have truly broken my heart."

"McKinley, you have given me everything but happiness." I thought maybe I wanted to shed tears for him—for us, but it would have been a waste.

❋❋❋

Passion finally entered the parlor, scrambling to pour my tea. As she reached for the teapot, I grabbed her by the arm, "Gal, didn't you hear me calling for you?"

Providing me with some resistance, Passion came back with, "I was helpin' Katie, ma'am. She had jes lost her husband, and…"

"You think I give a damn about that girl and that boy? When I call you, I expect you to be here. Do you understand?"

"Yessum."

"Now pour my tea and prepare that saucer with biscuits for me." I watched her, as I had done so many times before, and was made weak by her beauty. "Why don't you sit down and have a spot of tea with me?"

"No, thank you, miss. I has some chores to get done."

Passion and I hadn't many conversations since she'd been on the plantation, and I thought it time to make things crystal clear. "As a servant, you have no options here, Passion. You see what happened to January."

"That was not right, for Master to do that to Katie."

"And you think he and I care about how you feel? I got a good mind to take you down to the shed and give you five lashes so we can have an understanding!"

"You will do no such thing to her," McKinley said to me, coming into the parlor. "She is right. I should have put up a fight for January."

"Ignore his rants, gal. He's not in his right mind."

My husband invited himself to our little tea party and poured himself a cup of tea. "Passion, your missus got you living better than the others, and I bet she's trying to make you think she treats you better. The fact of the matter she only thinks of herself and doesn't care about anyone but Lizzie."

"Passion, you are dismissed. You and I will finish talking later." I observed McKinley watching every move Passion made, and it made my stomach turn. Her hands, her legs, her whole body, he kept his eye on her until she left. "What do you want, McKinley? You're becoming a bit of nuisance."

"I need to know why you married me. You were the reason I got up in the mornings. You made me feel whole."

"Oh, put a sock in it. No need to pour the bullshit on any thicker. I married you because you needed me, and I knew you would move heaven and earth for me. I've never had that. Not from my father, not from my mother, and sure as hell not from my last husband."

With all my heart, I never wanted to hurt McKinley, but the timing of his rant was perfect. "I will not ask you to leave, but I will ask you to keep your affairs separate from mine."

"I can live with that, but I have something to ask as well."

"What is it?"

"You must stop your late night visits to Passion. I hope you do not think that I did not know because I know everything that goes on around here." McKinley did not give me an answer. "Did you hear me?"

In his eyes that had grown weaker by the days, I saw his displeasure with my request. He rose from his chair, perused the room and then smiled devilishly. "Lizzie, my dear, don't forget how you got to such a place. Also, remember I can have you sent back to that last husband of yours that you abandoned. In my opinion, you have only been a guest here for the last twenty-five years."

22

McKinley and Passion

K nocking was not necessary because my visits had been welcomed. When I laid eyes upon her, all I wanted to do was run to her, but, on this day, she turned from me. "What's wrong, Passion?"

"You have taken one important man from Katie's life. Why did you do it, again?"

"What choice did I have? Lizzie and a whole army had me outnumbered."

"But those are *your* slaves and *your* land, and you let them come in here and take them from you."

She was right, but it was something I did not desire to dwell on. "What's done is done. You know I hate her."

"You should not. It is not God's way for us to hate."

"Passion, how I am supposed to feel? She has used me and made me look like an imbecile." There was a way about this young girl that filled my heart with warmth and compassion, and, unlike it would have in most White men I knew, those desires did not reach my loins. Since the day she read those letters to me, I was connected to her. She saw my pain as my ignorance had been magnified on paper.

"It has been a long day, and I am tired. I want to get up a little earlier than usual, so I can go to Katie's house and help her with the children. I saved my meals from the latter part of the day to give to her."

I was not ready to go home, and I wanted to spend more time with her. "Would you mind terribly if I lie down next to you? I just need..." Complaining of yet another headache, Lizzie had consumed two glasses of wine and gone to bed.

"No need to explain," she said softly.

A question to which I needed to know the answer was on the tip of my tongue, but I was afraid to ask, knowing I would frighten her and cause her to take her affections away. As I rested in her arms, I realized that if anyone discovered us, life would never be the same. My interests heightened in knowing from whence this being came. "Tell me..." Then without warning, there was an excruciating pain radiating from the crown of my head. Before I could turn around, I was jabbed in the head again with what felt to be a large rock. I rolled onto the floor from the bed, holding my skull, which felt as if it was split. "Lizzie, oh God no," I pleaded. Blood gushed from my wounds while my wife stood in the puddle and delivered a final blow.

"Please stop! You will kill him," Passion screamed, jumping to her feet and rushing to my side. "He only needed a friend! He only needed a friend!" she whimpered. Her tears fell from her cheeks and into my face. Faded impressions of what love really should have felt like soaked themselves into my soul for eternity.

❊❊❊

When I tried to help Master, the missus backhanded me and sent me falling to the floor, but I got up and went back to his side. He had done nothing to hurt me or humiliate me for as long as he had known me, and, for that, I was grateful. Never once had he looked upon me as filth or with lust in his eyes. "What have you done?" I asked solemnly as I held his bloodied head in my lap. "He did nothing wrong."

Missus had a fire in her eyes that blazed as she looked upon her crime. Slowly, I watched the flames burn out, seeing that she was quickly realizing what she had done. "You have been letting him have his way with you."

"No, miss, you're wrong. Us…"

"Shut your mouth! I know you're with child. I see your belly growing, and I see it in your face. He has made you his whore, and you turned him against me."

Before I could answer, Katie burst into the house, "Passion, I…" She froze in her steps.

"And what are you doing here?" Missus inquired. "Was he fucking you, too?"

"No, miss, I comes up to jes sit and talks with Miss Passion," she said, kneeling next to me.

"Well, ain't no time for talkin' right now. You two are goin' to help me get him out of here."

I never knew a dead man could be so heavy. Katie brought me a blanket from the bed, and I put his head upon it. "Ma'am, us can't carry him all by ourselves. Us gone need some help," Katie told her.

Missus dropped the red-stained rock and ordered us to leave Master where he was on the floor. I did not want to leave him, for the one thing he desired was to not die alone.

Covered in blood, I said, "Miss, us can't leave him here. He should be buried."

She walked around his body, like she was proud of what she

had done. "You're right. We should bury him. Come quickly and help me take off this dress." Katie and I helped Missus out of her dress and hoop, leaving only her petticoat. Nobody but me knew she always wore a pair of boots, which is why it seemed like she was always stomping ants into the earth when she walked. She picked Master up by the shoulders of his jacket, and, with the strength of two mules, she dragged him from the house.

"Just follow me," she ordered.

We stopped by the barn to get a shovel. I don't know where Missus got that strength from, but she took his body almost two miles down the road. Halfway down, she asked me and Katie to help because she said her back was hurting her real bad. The curls that normally sat on top of her head had fallen into her face and were sticking to her skin, which glistened with sweat. When we arrived at the place she wanted to be, she handed the shovel to Katie and told her to start digging. As the dirt flew up and then fell back to earth, I asked God for His forgiveness.

❁❁❁

Katie and I walked back to the house in silence. I do not think either of us knew what to say. Missus walked about six steps ahead of us; like she was trying to beat the sun. I got to the house, expecting her to come in and get her dress, but she went on to the big house instead. A while later, she stormed through my front door.

"So do you hate me, too?"

Her hair was still wet from an apparent bath as she smelled

of fresh roses and scented talcum powder. Surprisingly, she had dressed herself in a very simple outfit absent of a hoop and petticoat and was barefoot. My immediate thought was that she had gone mad. It was evident she had been somewhere close by, listening to my and Master's conversation from the night before.

"God does not want us to hate."

"He doesn't want us to kill either, but it happens."

I wanted her to leave. "Is dare sumthin' you need from me, Miss? I wus in the middle of gettin' myself ready to come and get breakfast for you."

"Well, there is." She smiled wickedly. "I want you to get your things and come with me. I'm movin' you into the house." Asking her for what reason would have been the death of me, so I went to the corner and got my bag. "What's in there?" she asked.

It was none of her business, but I chose to answer. "Those is thangs my mother gives to me. I always keeps dem with me."

"Oh." There was a man standing at the front door of the big house knocking like he thought somebody was home. I pulled the spread from my bag and gave it to her so she could cover herself. "May I help you, sir?"

He was a dignified looking man with a clean suit, bowtie and hat on. "Good morning, ma'am, my name is Tom Griffin, and I'm looking for Mrs. Lisbeth Brown Wellsworth."

"That's me."

"Very well, I have a letter for you," he stated, handing her an envelope. "You have a good day."

Missus examined the outside of the letter first and then handed me the spread back. "Go and fix my breakfast, while I take this letter in the study. By the way, you are to put your things in the room with me. That is where you shall sleep from now on."

23

LIZZIE

Oh, *sweet Jesus, what have I done?* I killed him. When I saw him laying there with Passion, I can't explain what rushed through me. My feelings intensified when I thought of him touching her. I had seen them many times at night together, and, while my instinct as a wife should have been to be angry with her for imposing upon our lives, I was angry with him for touching and loving on something that was mine. For months I had watched Passion and found I desired her. Having never felt that way about another woman, particularly a servant, I sent my emotions into a hatred toward McKinley for not being the man he should have been to keep me from even thinking about her that way. She is having his child, and I will be forced to live with it in my house because to keep from being spoiled again, she and that child of hers will always remain with me. McKinley had done nothing but try to love me, but no matter what he did, I could not give it back.

❋❋❋

Waiting for Passion to bring my breakfast, I sat down and read the letter from the past I had tried desperately to forget.

Dear Lisbeth:

I hope this letter reaches you and finds you in good health. Oh, how I have truly missed you! I have looked over every hill and meadow to find you. Many letters have come back to me, but I wanted to try one last time. Since you left Georgia, so much has transpired with me. The day you arrived to tell me you were leaving I was hoping to be able to share some news with you. I was experiencing the love of my life, and I wanted my best friend to know about it. First, let me tell you it was not Royce. Instead, I never thought I would call a man beautiful, but this one was. He knew how to love me, and he gave me the attention Royce did not. His attention was so captivating that I feel in love with him and bore his children, Amelia and Quincy. This man, you know him. He is Josiah. To protect Josiah and Quincy, my mother took them to Massachusetts to be with my Aunt June. I was forced to raise Amelia in a cave that the servants had built at the edge of the plantation. It took some twenty years for Royce to discover my secret. Needless to say, he was livid and tried to end my life. I have not seen him since. A short time later my mother returned to Georgia and found the servants that had been loyal to her had taken me under their care and nursed my injuries. She took me back to Massachusetts with her where I recovered and was finally able to live in peace with my son and my Josiah. The servants told me Royce killed Amelia, but I find that hard to believe because I still feel there is a part of me out there somewhere.

I hear you married well this time around, and I indeed pray you have finally found happiness. Josiah, when he came here to Massachusetts, took the knowledge he had gained and joined the state legislature. Despite my displeasure about it, he, along with Quincy, has joined in the fight for the freedom of those he had left behind. I miss them so. I do not know what my life would be like if anything ever happened

*to him. I am sure you do not wish to hear this, but I hope the North
wins this fight, so I can return to Georgia with my family to claim
what is rightfully ours.*

Lisbeth, I wish you well and anticipate hearing from you soon.

All my love,

Annie Few

I always figured she would marry a nigger, and I felt like I'd
achieved something because I was finally better than her. I
couldn't wait until Royce came back so I could share with him
that Annie was alive.

❁❁❁

Months passed, and I began to quickly realize the absence of
a man around the house was a complication that affected everything we did. The ones that had been able bodied and knew how
to pull up the rear whenever January wasn't around were off with
Royce. There were many days I had to sit on McKinley's horse
to watch over the fields. With the state of things, no one was
really buying much tobacco, and I knew we were losing money.
Many of the merchants had closed their shops, and some simply
didn't want to work with a woman. Our exports stopped, I believe,
as punishment for us being in the South and using slave labor.

Since Passion moved into my bedroom, I'd had to deal with
a particular set of emotions I'd never experienced. I began thinking things I never thought I'd think, and then, I began doing
things I never thought I'd do. On an evening when I was nursing
a headache, I retired earlier than usual. When I got to bed, I
tossed and turned but couldn't fall asleep. I kept thinking of

Passion. I got up and paced the floor until I broke into a sweat. After hours of waiting for her to come to bed, I heard her footsteps in the hallway and took a seat in a chair next to the dresser. She struck a match to light the lamp, and that's when she saw me sitting there naked.

"Ma'am?" She looked at my body first, then into my eyes.

My body temperature was causing water to run down my chest and between my thighs. "Did I startle you?"

"Well, yes, ma'am. I thought you had went to bed already." Her belly was growing bigger by the day, and her beauty was still remarkable. She slept on a bed across the room from mine that the other servants envied. I'd taken pillows and sheets from the other beds in the house and had given them to her to keep her comfortable. Previously when she had undressed, I made it a point to respectfully look away, but, for several weeks, I found myself staring at her plump figure. Tonight, I looked at her with no shame or indignation. Before she slipped into her nightgown, I shifted my eyes to the beauty between her legs.

"Wait, Passion, before you get dressed."

"Yes, ma'am?"

I got up from the chair and carefully approached her with my hands in position to clutch her body at every curve I could. Her breasts were firm, and the curves in her body fit my palms perfectly. "I want you to relax," I said delicately. I slid my fingers between her thighs that she seemed to squeeze tighter and tighter the more I tried to get in. I placed my hand in the small of her back and gently pushed her into me to allow my fingers to find their place. The straight, black hair that covered the entrance into her inherent jungle tickled the skin around my fingers as I ventured into the land of the mystique. My breathing became heavier when I heard her gasp from my entry. I gazed into her eyes and received an unnerving glare from her. I wiggled my fingers and created motions I never realized I knew. For several moments she resisted me. To my surprise, I watched her empty glare became a reflection of ecstasy as she began to move her body in rhythm with the motion of my fingers. Her sporadic gasps turned into consistent moans. In my lifetime, I believed I'd never lay my lips upon one whose skin was not the color of mine, but it quickly became something I could not resist. Passion held her lips firm, not parting them a single bit to receive me. Seeing I was not giving up, she eventually gave in and combined the movement of her lower body with my wet forces. In that moment, we no longer existed as mistress and servant but as lovers.

The following morning I awoke to find Passion already out of bed, and I considered deeply what happened between me and her. I knew I loved her but could not determine to what degree. Feeling renewed, I walked over to where her bed was and lifted her pillow to my nose, inhaling her scent. I rubbed my hand across the sheets and imagined her silken skin against them; with me next to her. The bag she often carried with her was sticking out from beneath the bed, and I felt I had every right to go through it. Upon opening it, I immediately recognized the bedspread my father had given my mother. I vaguely recalled having given it to Annie. Something weighted was in the bottom of the bag, and I reached as far I could to grab hold of whatever it was. I pulled the item from the bag, along with a folded piece of paper.

Downstairs, I found Katie sitting next to Passion, who was crying and holding the bottom of her stomach. "What's goin' on here?"

"Da baby is comin', Miss. Us needs to git a doctor right 'way."

I walked to Passion and lifted the hem of her dress. Again, our eyes met. "I don't think there's time to get the doctor here. The baby's head's damn near sittin' in her lap."

We moved her to the bedroom where the pain became more constant as her body continued expelling McKinley's seed. While I pulled the baby's head out, Passion's tears became steady as she complained the pain wasn't getting any better. The baby, a little girl, came out, entering the world as a fighter with a set of lungs that could be heard up to Fort Monroe. "It still hurts so bad. Please make it stop," she begged. I didn't know what to do, but I noticed there was something else coming out of her.

"Katie, I think there's more than one. I need you to help her push," I directed. Passion pushed and matched each effort with a loud cry. Within seconds, another little girl entered the world. Even though she was exhausted, Passion asked to see the babies, but Katie and I were both standing there in my bedroom trying to figure out why one of them was pale white like McKinley, and the other was the color of honey. There was no mistaken it had been a full day for me, and it was only a sign of things to come. Passion slept well into the night and awoke to find Katie and me each holding a baby.

Sitting up in the bed, Passion asked, "Can I see?"

Grinning from ear to ear, Katie answered, "You got two uh dem, Miss Passion. Two purdy little girls."

While Passion had been sleeping, I looked at both girls and didn't see any resemblance to McKinley. For a brief moment, they opened their eyes. One had blue ones, and the other had brown, with no explanation to anyone but Passion as to why. I, too, realized I'd killed my husband for something he actually may not have done. "That light one looks a little like McKinley, don't you think?" I asked.

Passion glanced over at Katie, who was singing to the bundle she was cradling. Obviously humiliated, she said, "Ma'am, maybe we can talk about this later. I give you anything you want, if you just let me rest a little bit. Afterwards we can talk all you want."

In exchange for more moments like what we'd already had, I agreed and left it alone.

24

PASSION

I had never had a friend until I met Katie, and I was going to protect what we had. I am not going to say I have been comfortable with the things Missus and I do, but there have been times when I did what I needed to do to just hear her say she would set me free one day. Every morning I go to the icehouse to get ice for breakfast and then I go back for lunch. I got there one afternoon and found Missus sitting in there waiting on me. Words between us were few, and this time was no exception. Missus hopped onto the table I used to chop ice and pulled her dress up in front of me. She did not have on any undergarments. Instantly, I was taken back to the night the slave catcher had caught up with me and how his head had rolled back toward the sky when I had touched him with tongue and lips.

Standing in front of Missus, I leaned in to her and asked the Lord for his forgiveness—a second time. Missus slid her body toward me with her dress still raised. I lowered myself to where I faced the graying hair of her private spot. Times before, it had been pressed up against me or wrapped around my fingers. It had never occurred to me that a woman could experience the same passion a man could when stimulated by the power within. I encircled my tongue in and around the split until I felt Missus's body jerk a little. She muttered words to me that I could not understand. She grabbed my head and pushed it deeper into her cave. My swirls landed in the depths of her walls, jabbing the hole with my tongue and following it with soft, swift movements across the tiny mountain that protruded from her opening. "I love you," she shrieked. "Passion, I love you."

❂❂❂

Honey Marie and Dottie Ann were the joy of Missus's life. The war went on around us with none of us knowing how the other side was fairing. Missus suggested one afternoon that she go into town to pick up some things for the babies and to talk once again with one of the merchants about doing business with her. Bouncing Honey back and forth in my arms, I stood at the window and watched the carriage leave the grounds. I had grown tired of the life Missus was forcing me to live. I cannot say I did not love her because I had never experienced it to know what it was supposed to feel like. I will say, though, that I wanted my freedom. Despite what she and I shared in bed, it never changed the fact I was her slave, and, until Negroes were free, that was the way it would always be. I started looking through some drawers in the bedroom, and I came upon a letter addressed to Missus. I recognized the handwriting immediately and opened the envelope.

That night, I lay in the bed next to her and felt nothing. I did not want her touching me or even looking at me. She was, indeed, the horrid woman McKinley told me that she was. Atop a stack of fluffed pillows, I took a fleeting look at her while she read the newspaper. "Do you really love me?" I asked.

I know she had to notice the fluidity in my speech, for I realized it was time for everyone to come clean. Turning to face me, she replied, "I do."

"If that is so, then why have you not told me that you knew my mother was alive?"

Missus seemed to have anticipated the question because she answered without fail. "I guess we've both been snooping." She then opened the drawer next to the bed and pulled out the gold trinket box. "Where did you get this from? And the bedspread?"

"My mother."

"And how do you know I know your mother?" I could not answer. Despite the war, the slave codes were still in effect. "I didn't think you would answer because you can read, and that's why you slip in your language with me. You've walked around here all this time being dishonest."

Angry, I interjected, "You have been the liar here. You have held me here, promising me everything but my freedom. If you know who my mother is, then you too know that I am not, by law, a slave. Had you really wanted to be true to me, you would have let me go the minute you realized that."

Missus was red in the face with rage. "I'm not going to argue with you. You can leave, if that's what you want to do, but those children will stay with me."

"What? Are you mad?"

Missus rose from the bed and put on her robe. "Passion, Amelia, whatever your name is, you and I both know those children are the bastard children of your close friend's husband, but neither of them know it. If you wish to keep it that way, then you will stay here with me and the children."

Katie would be hurt beyond words, and, while I agreed to stay, I reminded Missus, "Remember God sees everything; especially when we tell nothing."

25

LIZZIE

Thinking about how I was going to explain McKinley's absence to Mavis never entered my mind. In the beginning, none of us thought the war would last as long as it had, and there came a time when Mavis decided to move to Richmond to fulfill his political obligations. He came to visit toward the end of July in1863.

"Miss, Marse Mavis's carriage is pullin' up outside," Katie warned when she saw me coming downstairs.

"Oh, really?" I know she was surprised to see me so calm.

"Miss, iz dare sumthin' you needs fer me to get fer you or him?"

"Nothin' for me. Make sure he has somethin' cool to drink."

The war had aged Mavis as he had grown a white beard that touched the middle of his chest. He'd put on a little weight and was using a cane to help him get around. The ol' bastard walked in the door bitchin'. "All these damn niggers around here, and I have to open a door for myself?"

President Lincoln had signed the Emancipation Proclamation earlier in the year, and I had given most servants the chance to leave. Many left while only a handful stayed.

"Suh." Katie curtsied.

He never acknowledged her. "Well, Mavis Crump, what brings you here?" I asked.

"I been up at Fort Monroe a lot these days. The Yanks run the damn place. They even got it to where if a nigger runs away and manages to get down there, then they won't send them back to their owners. They got niggers coming from every which way trying to get there. The niggers even got their own infantry now. Fifty-third...fifty-forth Massachusetts something. It makes all this work McKinley did around these parts worth nothing. Speaking of him, where is he?"

Katie and Passion waited patiently as I gave them the signal to leave the room. "Mavis, McKinley passed away last year. We tried to reach you, but, with you moving around all the time, we didn't have any luck."

Mavis paused for a moment and took a long sigh. Clearing his throat, he asked, "What happened?"

"He died in his sleep. Went to lie down to take a nap and never woke up."

"I see." Mavis was clearly devastated, and I was uneasy because I was unprepared for his visit, especially when the questions started. "Where'd you bury him? Is he in the cemetery just over the hill?"

For as long as I had known Mavis, I hadn't liked him, and it had become more than evident that he suspected something. "He didn't want to be buried out there."

"I find that hard to believe, Lizzie. Where else would he have wanted to be buried?"

I refused to let him back me into a corner. "Look, I'll have Passion or Katie take you to where he is. But first you have to tell me about his will and what's in it. It's been hell around here since that blasted war started."

Mavis didn't want me to see his tears, but I heard them when his voice cracked. "Legally, I'm going to need proof he's dead before I can tell you anything."

"Proof? What kind of proof? Hell, he's dead," I insisted.

"Show me where he's buried then."

"I told you those gals in there will take you to him. What's in the will?"

"Well, quite naturally, his wife gets everything that was ever truly his—the land, the house, the slaves—all of it."

My eyes bulged from their sockets. "What do I need to do to make this happen? I've been waiting for months to hear this news."

Mavis reclined in his seat and looked at me the way he did the day I married McKinley and said, "You have never been his wife; therefore, you are entitled to nothing."

"What the hell do you mean?"

"Friends are friends to the end, and that's likely why you haven't any. I tried to look out for McKinley all his life, but there was nothing I could do make him see you and your mother for who you really were. All those months you two thought I was working I really was, but I found time in between to do some investigating about you and your mother. You never divorced your husband, Will Brown—the tenant farmer—and, unless he committed some crime against you, you are still married, making any marriage to my deceased friend null and void. By order of the power invested in me by McKinley, you are to leave this place and never come back."

Reluctantly, I directed Mavis to the spot where McKinley was buried, but I never told him how he met his demise. "Miss, miss, come quick," Katie yelled anxiously from the courtyard. I could feel the rumble of the earth beneath me. I rushed to the window and saw a cloud of dust rising from the clearing. The army had returned, but it had more than tripled in size...

PASSION

When the dust settled, the large group of Negro soldiers and two Union armies under the command of Major General Benjamin Butler had ridden onto the plantation with many more Negro soldiers behind them. Missus and Mavis were both overwhelmed by the presence and stood speechless until Mavis conceded he no longer had an interest in the ownership of the plantation, telling them they could have whatever they wanted. Katie tried frantically to look over the heads of all the soldiers with hopes of finding January.

An older Negro man came forward on his horse and dismounted in front of me and Katie. Wearing his uniform proudly, he walked toward me, but I took two steps back "Good day, miss," he said respectfully as he removed his gloves so he could shake my hand. "My name is Colonel Josiah Montgomery of the 54th Massachusetts Regiment, and I am your father."

Something inside told me to believe him, but I looked to Missus and became afraid. "How can you say that? You don't know me."

Colonel Montgomery had to be most gentle man I had ever met. "Believe me when I say that I am. That woman over there knows this to be true. We used to play together when we were children."

I had many reasons to hate Missus, and I truly did not wish to add to the list. But I had to ask her, "Missus, is this true?"

She stood there holding Dottie with a shrewd expression; as if to quietly admit he was right. She handed me the baby and simply turned to walk away. "How did you find me here?"

"I told him." January smiled as he moved to the front of the group. "When us left here dat day wid Marse Royce, us fought baddles et Yerktown. Sum uh us coloreds got free and runned t'ward Fort Monroe. Us met up wid udders and said us wanted to fight to be free. Dat's whar I met Quincy, yer brudder."

"My brother? How..."

Colonel Montgomery interrupted, "Your grandmother, Risella, took Quincy and me with her to Massachusetts just after you two were born. To disguise who we were, we were given the last name of your great aunt and uncle. Quincy met January in South Carolina, and he kept telling your brother he knew someone that bore a striking resemblance to him but it was a woman. We have looked so long for you."

"Where is he now?"

"He's down in Georgia with Annie; preparing a homecoming for you."

❂❂❂

Back in Georgia, I, with my brother Quincy, inherited the land that had been cultivated by our grandfathers. The home my mother once shared with Royce had been destroyed, but the house has been rebuilt. The war ended in 1865, with Negroes being given their freedom. Lives were lost, and bonds were broken because of the South's obsession with slavery. Many before me, enslaved or not, lived and died without knowing love—whether it be for a man, a woman, a country—all of whom have ultimately paid the highest price for passion.

ABOUT THE AUTHOR

Divine destiny is what motivates mother, daughter, author, playwright Laurinda D. Brown to do what she does—write novels and plays that portray real people in true-to-life situations no different than your average neighbor next door. Brown explains, "Growing up in Memphis, Tennessee, and graduating from Howard University in Washington, D.C., exposed me to the varied and diverse sides of human nature. It also gave me the opportunity to observe people and their situations and try to discern what made them do the things they did. I realized that people are people. My writing helped me work through my own issues, emotions and circumstances. Writing expresses my take on the world." Before *The Highest Price for Passion* and her dramatic endeavor, *Walk Like A Man—The Play*, Brown began her literary journey with *Fire & Brimstone* (Strebor Books), the 2005 Lambda Literary Award finalist for "Best Debut Lesbian Fiction," followed by *UnderCover* (Strebor Books), and *Walk Like A Man*, the 2006 Lambda Literary Award winner for "Best Lesbian Erotica." She is a featured writer in Zane's anthology *Purple Panties*, and the new Nghosi Books anthology, *Longing, Lust, and Love: Black Lesbian Stories* and most recently penned *Strapped*, an urban novel about child sexual abuse and its effects on a young woman's sexuality. Laurinda resides with her two daughters in the greater Atlanta metro area where she is currently working on her next project.

EXCERPT FROM

UnderCover

BY LAURINDA D. BROWN
AVAILABLE FROM STREBOR BOOKS

MISS NAY'S REVUE

Patrick sat at the bar waiting for the love of his life. The house was packed as usual with folks in from Atlanta and St. Louis for the holiday weekend. Cars were lined up on both sides of Front Street that night—which wasn't a big deal to many. But, to Patrick, it meant the world.

It meant that everyone had come out to see his baby perform at the club. Men from all walks of life handed Patrick's lady dollar bills, five-dollar bills, ten-dollar bills, and, on the first of the month, maybe even some twenties. But none could surpass Patrick. Every Saturday night, dressed to the nines, he would watch those other men walk to the front of the stage, fanning bills and pieces of paper with phone numbers scribbled on them. Often tripping over themselves to do it, some even borrowed from their dates just to be able to touch the silken hands of The Menagerie's biggest star. But it was Patrick who made a hush fall over the crowded room. Leaving his double B-52 and Lite Beer, he rose from his VIP booth and pulled out his Coach breast wallet that Nay had gotten for him while on a trip to California. He was seductively smooth, suave, and anything else that a gay Black man with the most amazing smile and the whitest teeth could ever be. Fragranced with imported cologne and always clad in custom suits, Patty was the center of attention. With every stride—waving that bill in his hand, eyes followed him, wondering what dead president he'd pulled from his wallet. By the time he reached the stage, the bill was creased across Ben Franklin's face, gently resting on his index finger. And Miss Nay? She would lean over and smile as her man first kissed the paper and then placed the crisp one hundred-dollar bill between her breasts.

Tonight, though, Patrick was not all right. He didn't get his usual table in the center of the dance floor and, knowing he wouldn't be staying long, he didn't bother to remove his jacket. Instead, he sat slumped over the bar and nursed a flat ginger ale that had succumbed to the three ice cubes that the bartender had so graciously offered. He hadn't been to the club in over two months.

About that fact folks had begun to talk. "Patty, you wan-anotha drink?" someone offered. But Patrick remained silent and kept swirling his straw around the bottom of his glass. "Guess not," snorted the waitress as she sashayed her way to the other end of the bar. Patrick sat practically stock-still with his back turned to the stage. The frigid air around him warned the usual passersby to stay away, to stay far away.

Three years seemed barely like three days to Patty, for he and Miss Nay were lovers at first sight. They'd traveled the world together: Cancun, Montego Bay, Paris, and London. Patty insisted that Nay allow him to occasionally get his dick sucked by nameless strangers, and she was assured things would go no further. In exchange for that luxury, Nay was given the world, and she flaunted it. But privilege came with a price that Nay didn't mind paying. She wasn't allowed to take anyone home with her, nor was she allowed to accept phone numbers or business cards. Those weren't the club's rules. They were

Patty's. As she performed, Miss Nay electrified the crowd with her sultry moves and finesse, but outside of work Nay was strictly off limits. Everybody knew that. That was the way Patrick wanted it.

Patrick, with long and lovely supermodel eyelashes, sat with sullen eyes, agonizing over what he'd finally gotten the nerve to do. Closing his eyes, he whispered to himself, "Now, let's practice this one more time." With the music blaring at deafening levels from one corner of the club to the other, no one heard him thinking out loud. *Take a breath.* "Nay, Baby, you know that I love you more than life itself. Nothing else in this world mattered to me when we were together. I allowed everyone and everything to come second to you and me, and at times, that even included my family. Since Mama died, the whole world has been looking a lot different to me. Those things that didn't matter before mean a whole lot now, and I've got to do the right thing. My family is expecting it, and so is God. I promised Mama on her deathbed that if she would just surrender to Him so that she could finally be free of her pain, then I would dedicate my life to serving Him and would leave *this* life alone. The things that I chose to turn the other cheek to have come around and smacked me in the face. I can't continue to act like the world around me is grand when my insides are about to fall out. Every time I think about you, touch you or kiss you I feel like I'm dissing Mama. So, every time I get that way—the devil's way—I go to church. I've been scrubbing the floors, cutting the grass, cooking in the kitchen—anything to keep me from thinking about you. The next thing I knew I'd found my way into the pulpit and realized that I had something to say. I mean it's like my soul just opens up when I'm there. All these people around me…hundreds of them, and, with all that, I still feel like it's just me and God. When I'm there, I like what I see. I like what I feel." Even with his voice rising at times to octaves just above a whisper, it seemed as if no one had heard a word Patty uttered. He continued, "Nay, I realize now that love is more than just what we have. It's more than what I ever thought we had. The last thing that I've ever wanted to do was to hurt you, but, after all these weeks of Sunday School, Bible study, and worship services, I now know that life is about the choices you make, and right now…today, I have to choose God."

Patty's heart transformed his emotions into tears that flooded his eyes and overflowed down his cheeks. And just when he'd reached the point of locking out all else in the club around him, just when he'd felt there was no one else in the room but him and God, Patty opened his eyes amazed and bewildered to see that there was also Miss Nay.

This epitome of refined elegance and style was exemplary of regal stature; yet this woman of grandeur, this mega diva worthy of applause until her last breath, simply sat there, and, with her now former lover, shed the same tears. She shared the same pain. The once flawless make-up was carelessly smeared, revealing the mustache fuzz and facial hair. Nay, displaying divine class and stature to the end, slowly removed the silk scarf that had been a gift from Patty. Speechless, Nay gently reached for Patty's cheek and tenderly kissed it. She draped the scarf around Patty's neck, rose from the bar stool, and dejectedly strolled towards the dressing room to gather her things. There would be no more encores. This was her final curtain call.

Once out the club door, it would be the first time in years that she would have to face the world as Nathaniel Chamberlain Alexander.

MAINTAINING THE CONNECTION

MOCHAMD: Hi

CreolSista: Hey you. Long time no see ;)

MOCHAMD: Not true. You saw me exactly 19 hours and 47 minutes ago. Sorry for being late. Had to work an extra shift last night.

CreolSista: Never thought anyone could work more than me.

MOCHAMD: I know. It's always good, though, to come home, sign on and see you here. Makes it all worthwhile. I have a surprise for you.

CreolSista: ;) What is it?!

MOCHAMD: How's everything? How are you?

CreolSista: What's my surprise? And stop changing the subject!

MOCHAMD: LOL ;)

CreolSista: Okay! Okay! I'm doing well. Work is good, and everyone here is doing okay. Getting ready to go out of town.

MOCHAMD: Out of town? Again?

CreolSista: Yes, again. A combination of work and vacation. Mostly vacation, though. I was waiting until everything was confirmed before saying anything to you.

MOCHAMD: Well, darn!

CreolSista: ???

MOCHAMD: My surprise was that he and I were actually coming there for a month. He wants to take a look at some real estate to redevelop, and I was hoping to get a chance to finally meet you. When do you leave?

CreolSista: Ummm, next Thursday. I'm planning to be gone for almost two months.

MOCHAMD: Now that's what I call a vacation! I don't think that we even leave for another three or four weeks. Any chance you'll be back a little early?

CreolSista: It depends on how things are going. I've been working nonstop for the past two years, and some down time would be wonderful. The university is on break, too, so I just decided to take some vacation time as well. The kids are out of school for a few weeks, and even though it's beautiful here, a change of scenery would be nice.

MOCHAMD: Well, maybe the trip back will get delayed, and I'll still be there when you return. It would be great to meet you.

CreolSista: Same here. You have my phone number and address. Use it for a change!

MOCHAMD: I will. I promise.

CreolSista: So. How are things at home?

MOCHAMD: Better, I guess. He's probably never going to change. Business comes first, then him, and then me.

CreolSista: Lemme ask you something.

MOCHAMD: What?

CreolSista: Are you happy?

MOCHAMD: Yes.

CreolSista: Liar.

MOCHAMD: What?

CreolSista: If you were happy, you wouldn't get so much joy from chatting with me. You might be content, but you're definitely not happy.

MOCHAMD: I resent you saying that.

CreolSista: So, it's the truth. You have no idea what you're getting yourself into.

MOCHAMD: How about we change the subject?

CreolSista: You know, I'm not surprised. You always want to do that when you're about to be outed.

MOCHAMD: Anyway, do you realize we've been chatting for almost three years now?

CreolSista: ;)

MOCHAMD: You actually mean a little something to me.

CreolSista: A little?

MOCHAMD: Okay, a lot then. I get butterflies whenever I see you here.

CreolSista: Trust me, the feeling is mutual. I'm about to start my day while you're ending yours.

MOCHAMD: I like that feeling, too.

CreolSista: And what feeling is that ;)?

MOCHAMD: Having you on my mind before I go to bed at night.

CreolSista: ;)

MOCHAMD: Do you feel the same way?

CreolSista: I do but with reservation.

MOCHAMD: Why the hesitance?

CreolSista: I have my reasons, but I don't want to get into them.

MOCHAMD: ;(

CreolSista: No need to pout about it.

MOCHAMD: Please tell me.

CreolSista: I'll admit that you bring something really special to my life. I think that we established that some time ago. "Seeing" you just as I'm about to face the day is really a nice feeling to have first thing in the morning.

MOCHAMD: That's all you have to say?

CreolSista: I don't know what else you're looking for me to say. I mean you're in a relationship…one that you've been in for quite some time. The flip side is that I'm not. I'll be almost whatever you want me to be for you, but for personal reasons, I have to protect me.

MOCHAMD: oic

CreolSista: As much as I like chatting with you, I'm still careful. You're practically married, so I know this will never go anywhere. We're both professional women with very busy schedules. C'mon now, let's be real. Where do you honestly believe this can go?

MOCHAMD: I don't know. I think that we have a connection that is worth maintaining. I do miss you when we're not talking, and, on those nights when "home" isn't all that it should be, I miss you even more.

CreolSista: Having said that, don't you think that you've got some things you need to work through?

MOCHAMD: I don't know.

CreolSista: Well, you'll have two months to work it out. It's getting late, and I have to run some errands before I go to work.

MOCHAMD: Now you're pissed.

CreolSista: A little bothered but not pissed. Got too much to do to be upset about this today. Let's face it. We've never met, and it doesn't seem like we ever will. We've only talked twice in a three-year period, and that's because I called YOU. I even wrote you a letter!

MOCHAMD: It's too hard to try to call you with him always scanning the phone bill with fifty thousand questions, and putting things on paper around here might not be such a good idea either.

CreolSista: Awfully damn funny you manage to find time to hop on here to chat with me when God-knows-who could walk in on you! So what's the difference?

MOCHAMD: That's not the point.

CreolSista: The point is that you're trippin' and that you've NEVER called or written. I'm tired of this being a one-sided whatever. We need a break. Gotta go.

MOCHAMD: I'll talk with you later?

MOCHAMD: Creol?

CreolSista is not currently signed on.

Amil sat and watched the computer screen waiting to see if CreolSista was going to sign back on. Amil knew she'd pissed her off. Their conversations had started off quite innocently. Amil had just been looking for some harmless company while Manney worked long hours at the firm. So one evening she perused the member profiles of BlackVoices.com and sent out about ten e-mails. She thought that it would be easy to keep up with e-mails from ten strangers, and it was likely that she'd only get two or three responses, if any at all. Five e-mails were sent to straight men—the harm in that was the possibility of them wanting more than just casual conversation. Four of the messages were sent to straight women—maybe one of them would be in search of the same thing: a little attention while the man in her life was away. But then there was the last one, sent to a woman whose sexual preference was listed as, "That's my business." She, CreolSista, was the only person that had responded. For three years, Amil had nurtured this Internet relationship because it had provided a consistent outlet from Manney's selfishness. CreolSista knew when to ask if anything were wrong at home. She knew when to stop asking questions once MOCHAMD's answers had become short and snappy. She knew when to give a virtual hug when a real one wasn't possible. A kind word, an eCard, or maybe even just a simple smiley face was enough for Amil to know that somebody else loved her, and, those simple tokens of thoughtfulness had won Amil's heart, mind, and soul. Getting up the nerve to exchange addresses and phone numbers with a complete stranger took a little while, though. For all she knew, the screen name could have been a man disguised as a woman or could've more easily been a serial killer. Never hiding who she was, CreolSista had made being loved by a stranger so easy for Amil. The two times that CreolSista had called she'd greeted Amil with "This is CreolSista." Their conversations lasted only a minute or two and had never gotten any deeper than the usual pleasantries. CreolSista, always on the speakerphone, had made it a point to be too busy to really talk but not too busy to stop and say hello. The intrigue kept Amil wanting more.